The Grev Ghost

The Grey Ghost

A Novel of Suspense

Colleen Affeld

Writer's Showcase
presented by *Writer's Digest*
San Jose New York Lincoln Shanghai

The Grey Ghost
A Novel of Suspense

Writer's Showcase
presented by *Writer's Digest*
an imprint of iUniverse.com, Inc.

For information address:
iUniverse.com, Inc.
620 North 48th Street, Suite 201
Lincoln, NE 68504-3467
www.iuniverse.com

This book is a work of fiction. Names, characters, places and incidents are either the product of the author's imagination or are used fictitiously, and any resemblance to actual persons, living or dead, events, or locales is entirely coincidental.

Credit for Graphic: Beverly Affeld

ISBN: 0-595-12861-0

Printed in the United States of America

This book is dedicated to my brothers and sisters and our wonderful parents, Hugh and June. I'll love you forever. And, to my husband Keith and our children, Kerri, Jim, Wendy and Deanna. You are my life.

EPIGRAPH

"An evil man out of the evil treasure of his heart bringeth forth that which is evil."

List of Illustrations

Acknowledgements

I would like to thank my professors, John Ruff and Walter Wangerin, for sharing in class their vast knowledge in the creativity of writing. I appreciate their taking the time to work with me and assist me by critiquing and editing my efforts, but most of all for their encouragement and kindness. I will be forever grateful. I would also like to thank all my friends and acquaintances who read and gave their invaluable opinions, and for their confidence in me. Lastly, I would like to thank Keith and Deanna for their patience and love.

PROLOGUE

As the train gently screeched to a halt, the late afternoon sun strobed radiantly through its windows, its glare only allowing glimpses of the pine dotted countryside. The glistening sunrays danced inside the train car and their warmth surrounded me in total relaxation. I was home. A smile crept across my mouth. I loved my career as a reporter at the Atlanta Star, but even more I loved these brief escapes from all the hustle, bustle of the big city and the deadlines that pushed me all day long. I savored every moment in the welcoming arms of home and family, among the gently rolling countryside of Central Florida. This visit was actually going to be a working vacation. Reporting was exciting and paid the bills, but my first love was creative writing, and it was here in this familiar place I planned to begin my, "Great Novel." This familiar and seemingly quiet paradise, of orange groves, pine forests and sparkling waters was a well-spring of memories; most wonderful, but some, even after the passing of time were unthinkable and frightening. They seemed to come creeping back in the middle of the night in my dreams; untold stories of youth. Untold, until now. It had taken me thirteen years to come to terms with these memories, which now I decided I not only needed to, but wanted to remove from the dusty recesses of my mind and awaken them again, to become the heart and soul of my story. So, here I was, pen and pad in hand, ready to embark on a journey through the past. I just hoped I could do it justice after all this time.

"DeLeon," the Conductor's muffled voice came over the intercom.

Gathering my belongings from the overhead bin, I moved towards the open doorway of the train car, taking in a deep breath of sweet springtime; four o'clocks and magnolia. A chameleon scurried across the wooden planks startling me, yet bringing a smile and an instant blast from the past. Funny how a tiny reptile could start those images flowing from days so long ago. I thought, this was a good sign.

A firm hand suddenly grasped my shoulder, "Hey Scoop," my brother Bud's voice greeted me. "How's the big bad city kiddo?" My eyes filled with watery joy as Bud and I hugged. Of the four Cummins' children, Bud and I were like two peas in a pod. At least that's what Grandma Cummins always said. Most of the time, the occasion for such a comment from her wasn't meant in the most complimentary manner. But, that was okay. We never minded. We were alike in many ways; both full of adventure and plenty of mischief. We wouldn't have had it any other way. Life certainly was never boring at the Cummins' house; that was for sure. I missed Bud a lot since I left for Georgia. Our whole family was very close and we enjoyed every minute spent together now that we were all older and on our own. Buddy took my bags and carried them to his car, putting them in the trunk. Climbing in the car, with Buddy behind the wheel, and me in the passenger seat, we headed out of the sandy parking lot of the depot onto the river road, with windows rolled down and the radio filling the afternoon airwaves. I tossed my head back and let the afternoon breeze caress my hair. I felt like a kid again riding shotgun with my older brother.

"Hey, Cal. How about we make a quick stop before I take you to Mom and Dad's?" Bud asked. "There's something I need to show you." Without waiting for an answer, Bud turned the car to the right and started up the hill into the deep green pine forest; our old stomping grounds. I hadn't been out here in ages I thought, as we drove past the old Jackson House that our family had rented for a short while when I was nine years old. I was saddened to see the orange grove dwindling away. Bud told me it happened during the deep freeze five years earlier. The blossoms just couldn't handle the unusual cold temperatures. The sandy acres now made way for new homes.

We continued on until we were almost to the curve in the road, down by the canal that meandered up from the St. John's River. Bud pulled his car off onto the road's shoulder. By choice I hadn't been down any further than the Jackson house since that night thirteen years ago. A chill started up my spine. "Bud, what are we doing here?" I asked.

"Cal, just hold on," Bud said. "I thought if you were so all fired up to write that novel, you should see this first. After all, you're going to have to come here sooner or later aren't you to write the story? Cal?" Bud's eyes questioned me.

"I don't know Bud, I thought I was ready for this, but now, being here…"

"Cal, just look over there," Bud said softly, pointing out the window. I looked in the direction Bud pointed to see a beautiful marble archway over two coquina rock pillars. It was the entrance to the old colored cemetery. The cemetery had been transformed into a freshly sodded garden, full of red and pink azalea, and tiny white four o'clocks; their vine's climbing up freshly painted white trellises. The once lopsided and chipped headstones were now uprighted and whitewashed. An image of a contagious, pumpkin-toothed grin filled my thoughts as I read the engraved archway. "Isaac Washington Memorial Gardens". "Oh Buddy. Who did this? I can't believe it. It is so beautiful."

"I guess being on the City Council has its advantages," Buddy beamed.

"Isaac would be so proud," I told Bud. "He worked so hard here all his life as caretaker trying to make due with what he had to keep it up."

We got out of the car and walked the pine-mulched pathway through the cemetery, neither of us speaking for a time. It was beautiful and so peaceful here now. Yet, with all the changes, an overwhelming eeriness came over me, and there was no shaking it. Bud and I continued walking until we came to an immense mossed covered Oak, where we came to an abrupt stop. Glancing at Bud, I could tell by his expression that he was being pulled back into the past, as was I. At its base, the Oak's bark still bared a deep gouge, although now, slowly rotting away; a home for chipmunks and squirrels. My worst fears of being here, were now surfacing. Phantom faces in the night, frightened stares, like a veil of evil, somehow fell over us. How could this beautiful place have ever been such a dark, frightening world of violence and hatred. I closed my eyes somehow thinking it would stop the images flashing deep within them. The images kept on. Opening my eyes, I moved quickly away, down the pathway, trying to focus on the splendor of the gardens surrounding me now. Finding myself across the road I looked out over an old cattail pond. Staring down the ditchline, I spotted the rusted remains of an old car, an old Plymouth, silenced forever in the river muck. A rogue breeze came out of the north sending a shiver to my core. Closing my eyes again, I saw an old grey Plymouth, no longer pieces of broken rusted metal, with its interior stripped away. Now, clearly I saw it, headlights piercing darkness, moving quickly through the night, bumping and throwing anything in its path. It moved quickly; like a cat. Yes! A powerful lion, it's grill, sharp, gnashing chrome teeth, and headlights like eyes on fire, its engine screaming, cutting the stillness of a winter's night. A hand touched my shoulder, causing me to jump. Opening my eyes to Bud's staring back, for an instant I was thrust to the present. Then, standing there together, Bud's arm over my shoulder, the two of us mesmerized by the heap of metal in the ditch, were now, in our minds, transported into times past, remembering and sharing, what changed us both forever; as a nine year old girl, and a sixteen year old boy, two peas in a pod. The same bitter images embedded behind cool blue eyes. Remembering…

THE GREY GHOST

CHAPTER ONE

The South's blazing hot summer days had transformed into September's more tolerable ones, and sandals and fishing poles were traded for school books and toe-pinching oxblood loafers. I was beginning my fourth year at Jefferson Davis Elementary school that fall of 1958. It had been a memorable year, Cape Canaveral had shot off a real honest to goodness space ship; we got a brand new state by the name of Alaska; and the Dodgers and Giants baseball teams moved from the East Coast all the way out to sunny California. Our family of six had moved too. My family being, my parents Will and Kathryn Cummins, my big brother Bud, my two sisters, Lynn and Kate and of course myself, Cally, the youngest. With Bud and Kate being teenagers and all, our parents decided we needed more space. Rather, my sister Kate needed space. Me, Lynn and Kate shared a bedroom. Kate was going through a phase or something. Anyway, that's what Grandma Cummins said. Her phase caused her to be so contrary lately.

   Kate and I looked a lot alike. Everyone said we took after our dad, tall
as rails, blonde hair and narrow faces. All us kids had Dad's blue eyes.
Mom's were green as emeralds. I guessed we were divided up pretty fair
and square, for as much as Kate and I resembled Dad, Lynn and Bud
took after our mom. They had thick black naturally wavy hair, except
Lynn's had a touch of red highlights like Grandma's. She wore it in

braids because she hated the curls. Said she'd like to chop it all off in an Italian Boy hairstyle, like those girls in the fashion magazines Mom got. Lynn and Bud also were blessed with Mom's ready smile. It could light up a room. Lynn had Mom's quiet ways and quick wit too. Buddy did manage to get Dad's tallness. Seems he got the best of both and was handsome as a movie star. The girls just loved Buddy.

We said goodbye to our old house on Garfield St., in the small Florida town of DeLeon. My father had started building our new four bedroom on the land next to the first house. Until its completion we rented a house from a man our father worked with, Jack Jackson.

We lived in that house for only a few months, but by the time we moved back to Garfield St., it seemed as though it had been years. The rambling, two-story southern style, white frame house with its wrap-around porch and white pillars was like an extension of our rugged and sturdy landlord. Jack Jackson possessed a slow Southern drawl, that rose from deep within him, flowing outward surrounding him in rich bass tones. He was just a good old Southern boy. Us kids called him the Bee Man. He kept square white boxes of bee-hives in the grove out behind the house. Bud, said he looked more like one of those Cape Canaveral Astronauts in his white coveralls and hood with its thick netting across his eyes. The rest of us, were simply in awe of the big man as he collected honeycombs dripping with the sticky golden substance. We were all forbidden to venture near the hives for fear of stirring up some angry bees.

No one had to tell me twice. I had been on the receiving end of a bee's stinger the spring before, while in Miss Steward's third grade class. Sitting in the back of the classroom trying to remember if it was i before e except after c, or the reverse, two bees flew down the back of my dress from the open windows behind me. I was half undressed, slapping and screeching by the time I reached the classroom door, headed for the girl's room. I've never been able to figure out how anything so darn mean could produce something so sweet and tasty as the Orange Blossom honey that the Bee Man graced our breakfast table with so many mornings in that big white house.

CHAPTER TWO

One Saturday morning shortly after moving in, my sisters and I had finished our morning chores and went out to the porch to cool off.

"We live out in the boonies," Kate said, seating herself on the front steps of the porch, elbows on her knees, pressing her face between her hands. The front of the house stood amongst enormous oak trees. Their leathery leaf covered limbs shaded the yard keeping the house cool during the heat of the day. Long needle pine, that seemed to reach clean to the sky lined the edge of the property. Across the road a white sandy field gave root to rows of citrus trees, chock full of orange and yellow fruit. A railroad track meandered across the horizon, and curved out of sight where it crossed over a gator filled swamp near the river. The county road curved off the main highway from town just before the railroad crossing, and if you kept to that direction it went on past the River Grocery, the train depot, and then on down to the St. John's River. A narrower paved road jutted off to the left after the grocery and climbed a grade through a thick pine forest and on past the Jackson house.

"Nobody will ever come visit us out here. Shoot, they couldn't ever find us," Kate mumbled on.

"Hey, you've got us, what more could you need," said Lynn holding her hands out as if to embrace our older sister. Lynn walked over to a pillar encircled with green vine and tiny white flowers. "Just smell these four o'clocks, it's great out here," she said taking a deep whiff of their sweet fragrance.

"Right, that's how I want to spend my Saturdays, smelling flowers and…Cally Cummins, would you stop doing that," Kate snapped as I popped the green stem off a crimson Turk's Cap and stuck the end in my mouth.

"One of these days you're going to suck one of Jack Jackson's bees right down your throat," Kate warned me. I very methodically pulled off another stem and finished off some more of the sweet nectar; then, holding my throat, I fell choking and gasping to the porch floor below. For a little extra drama I stuck my tongue out the side of my mouth and gave one final kick. Lynn laughed, but Kate just squinted her eyes and said in disgust, "I'm not amused."

"Why don't we see if Mom will take us to the movies this afternoon. *Birth of a Nation* is playing and I have to watch it for history if I want some extra credit," Lynn told a grumpy Kate.

"What's it about?" Kate asked. "I'm not sure. Linda Bates says it's got a colored fella in it that's crazy and a killer," Lynn said her eyes bugging out.

"Oh, Linda Bates is full of it. Why would you have to see that for?" Kate said disgusted.

"Well, I don't know, I figure it must have to do with the Civil War because that's what we're studying," Lynn told her. "Miss Clark said it's a silent movie, no talking."

"Now that sounds real exciting," Kate said rolling her eyes until the blue almost disappeared.

"It's on before *Godzilla*" Lynn said in her persuasive voice.

"Oh cool, giant lizards eating everything in sight," I told Kate, "You'll love it."

"You're weird, Cally," said Kate. "Billy Carson will probably be at the show," Lynn coaxed.

"Well, count me out," I said, "Patty's coming over and we're going exploring."

"Cally, you better stay away from that old boathouse," Kate warned.

"Who said anything about going there? Did I mention that Kate?" I was tiring of her mothering.

"You don't have to say anything Cally. We know you. All you needed was for Bud to tell us to stay away from there and that was like flashing a red blanket in front of a bull. You just can't help yourself," Kate teased. "You do remember what Bud said, don't you?"

"Yeah, there's a crazy old colored man down there that chops up little kids. He and Larry Voight saw him. So how come they go down there so much, and how come he hasn't chopped them up into little pieces by now? I think they must have watched one of Miss Clark's silent movies too many times," I told Kate. "Why don't you just go to the movies and chase after boys and leave me be?" I said stomping back into the house to wait for Patty to come. It irritated the fire out of me when Kate knew exactly what I was thinking. She knew good and well a trip to the boathouse was too tempting for me to pass up.

CHAPTER THREE

Sunlight glistened on shiny metal fenders as Patty and I rode bikes down the narrow pavement towards the River Grocery. Small change clinked in our pockets in rhythm to the turning pedals. The afternoon breeze whispered through long pine needles and cooled my face as we sped along. When we reached the county road Patty stopped, "Well, would you look at that," she said pointing and asked, "Where do they think they're going?"

Big Mack trucks with long trailers that read, "Clyde Beatty Circus" on their sides passed by us. Behind the caravan of oblong trailers came trucks pulling huge cages on wheels; lions, bears, and elephants.

"Jack Jackson said the circus would be back here soon. They have a winter campground down by the train depot," I announced.

Locked behind big iron gates were a few cottages where some trainers and a foreman lived, and there were a couple barn like buildings for the animals. A big arch over top of the gates advertised in big bold letters "Winter Home of the Clyde Beatty Circus."

The menagerie passed and Patty and I rode on to our destination to spend our pennies, more concerned with candy than circuses at the moment.

Inside the grocery in rows of clear ginger jars was a smorgasbord of mouth waterin', lip smackin', tooth decayin', sugar delights just waiting for us. After many moments of great indecision we picked red candy lipsticks and vanilla Turkish Taffy. Handing Mrs. Ford, the owner, our pennies we hurried out front to devour our purchases. Sitting on two orange crates we stuffed our faces and listened to Mrs. Ford and Mr. Peterson shoot the breeze about the weather and politics, and whatever else adults talked about. Mr. Roy Peterson was the father of Hal Peterson, a cantankerous boy in our class at Jefferson Davis. Roy Peterson was the most disagreeable grownup I ever did see, and mean as a snake. Probably where Hal got his orneriness I decided as I wallowed a big chew of vanilla taffy in my mouth. I did feel sort of sorry for Hal once in a while for having a daddy like Roy Peterson. Like the day Patty and I was playing baseball with some boys up at the school yard, before my family moved. Shoot, bases were loaded and I was on third. I knew it was a sure run when Hal came up to bat. All we needed was one run to tie. Well, Hal's daddy sure made a mess of it all. Hal didn't see the white pickup pull up as he came to the plate, and he sure wasn't expecting what happened after the first pitch, which was a ball. I saw it coming and wanted to holler out, but before I could, Roy Peterson collared poor Hal around the neck cussing and carrying on at him about not doing all his chores. His daddy dragged him right off the field in front of everybody. Hal never joined us again for a ball game. Probably embarrassed half to death. After that Hal came to school with a blackened eye and a swollen lip. Everybody knew his daddy done it. But Hal denied it. Another boy, by the name of Robert Lee felt sorry for Hal and said he ought to tell Miss Rowell, our teacher what happened to him. Maybe she'd talk to his daddy. Well, Katie bar the door. Hal's fists started flying and he tore into Robert so darn hard he knocked the wind clean out of him. Miss Rowell grabbed hold of Hal by the ear and marched him down to the Principal's office. Hal wasn't in school for a couple days afterwards. Probably got another beating when he got home for fighting.

Bang! Patty and I jumped. I nearly choked on what was left of my taffy. Mrs. Ford scolded, "Now Roy, save the pieces, and don't go bangin' on my counter no more."

"Well, hell, Louise, somebody ought to put a stop to that old boy's high falootin' yankee ideas." Bang! We jumped as Roy Peterson hit on the counter again. The man sounded madder than a wet hen as he boomed, "If that son-a-bitch keeps stirrin' them people up there'll be big trouble, I guarantee you."

"Calm down there Roy, you're not gettin' no argument here," Mrs. Ford said.

"I'm telling you Louise, Little Rock had the right idea; close them schools down, and show them Communists in the Supreme Court that we Southern boys won't be pushed around," Mr. Peterson said. His voice got quieter, and Patty and I couldn't make out what was being said after that.

"Let's get out of here before he comes out." Patty suggested, "He gives me the creeps."

We walked over to our bikes just as the screen door creaked open and Roy Peterson swaggered out his upper lip snarled up like a rabid dog. As he opened the door to his pickup and climbed in I couldn't help noticing his cowboy boots. Rattler I'd say, what with their pearly white scales tinged in black. Squinty oval turquoise stones, peeked out like snake eyes on the sides. Patty and I watched as the white Chevy pulled away in a dusty fog. "There goes the meanest man in River County," Patty said.

"Hey, how about one of those tangelos I told you about," I said wanting to forget about Roy Peterson. We lifted our kick stands and peddled our bikes towards the Anderson's Grove, with our taste buds set for the juicy fruit.

Chapter Four

"I'm stuffed," said Patty wiping sticky citrus juice onto her pants. "Three's my limit," I said feeling a little nauseated after piling oranges on top of all that candy. We gathered up the rest of the orange balls and dropped them in the saddle bag of Bud's old Schwinn. Pushing the bikes through the soft sand, we headed back to the paved road.

"No Picking! $500.00 Penalty! Trespassers Will Be Prosecuted!" Patty read staring all bug-eyed at a sign nailed to a telephone pole by the road. We looked at one another and down at the bulging saddlebags. "We can't take these, we'll go to jail," Patty said with a hint of panic.

"We've already picked them! We didn't know! Wouldn't it be worse to just leave them here to rot? Besides," I said, "They'd have to catch us picking them first."

A car could be heard rounding the bend down by the old Colored cemetery. Looking down at our sticky orange stained clothes and, as if reading each other's minds, we pushed our bikes back into the grove, finding shelter behind a moss covered oak tree.

The car drove by slowly. Patty and I sat crouched perfectly still until the engine's noise was a safe distance down the road.

Patty said, "They were going awfully slow. You don't think they saw us do you? Do you? Hey Cally, where are you?"

"I'm over here. Come look what's over this barbed wire fence," I called.

"Oh no, I'm not going over there," said Patty. "You said Bud told you a crazy old colored man lives in that boathouse. My daddy says that all colored men carry six-inch switchblades. That's probably what he uses to cut up kids with," Patty went on.

"Has anyone ever known anybody he cut? Besides if a Colored man cut up any kids around here, he'd be in jail by now. Come on," I said as I crawled between the wires, careful not to catch myself on the rusted barbs. "Come on," I waved Patty on to follow. She did, hesitantly.

Patty gasped and jumped back, causing me to do the same. "What on God's green earth is the matter with you?" I asked looking in the direction of her dazed stare. A Chameleon hopped off a fallen tree branch in front of us and slithered across the sand through the weeds.

The sunlight was blinding as it glared off the tin roof of the boathouse. Its crusty wood plank walls blended with the cypress trees and scrub pine bark. A window was just above eye view so I moved an old bait box lying next to the building underneath it, so as to get a peek inside. Big Johnson boat motors lined a wood railing and tarp covered fishing boats were everywhere. Snowbirds who came south for the winter to fish for the large-mouthed Bass the river was famous for stored their boats here.

"I want a better look. Let's go around back to the dock," I said.

Stepping off the box we made our way through thick scratchy weeds and sandspurs to the dock. The blue-black water of the canal gently rippled in the sunlight and I pinched my nose to escape the oily smells of engines and dead fish.

"Well, nothing's here. Let's go," said Patty turning to leave.

"Shhh," I whispered, grabbing her arm with a firm jerk.

"What?" she said, and I muffled my hand over her big mouth, pointing towards the other side of the building. As we both craned our necks to peek around the corner, Patty saw what I was pointing at. There sat Bud and his friend Larry, bare feet dangling in the water. Next to them sat a slightly built colored man in old worn out denim overalls. They were all talking and laughing and smoking cigarettes. We couldn't hear what they were saying, but suddenly the colored man opened his mouth, baring a wide pumpkin toothed grin, and gave out with a belly laugh that shook his whole being, and slapped his leg. Bud and Larry were doubled up with laughter too. Patty backed up. "Buds smoking," she whispered as if I didn't have eyes to see for myself. "I'll bet your mom and dad don't know that," she said. "No wonder he told you that story about some crazy man. He didn't want you to find their secret smoking place," she kept on.

"Quiet! They'll hear you, Sherlock," I said, not in the mood to hear a sermon on the evils of cigarettes, which I knew was coming. Patty was Pentecostal and once her father made her brother Paul smoke a whole pack of Camels without stopping. He caught him smoking down by the elementary school playground after school. Paul puked his guts up, but Patty said it was his just punishment to keep him from going to the devil.

"Come on' let's get out of here before Bud sees us," I said, tromping back across the weeds to the grove fence. I picked up my bike that had fallen on its side and rolled it back towards the direction of the paved road with Patty trailing behind. The afternoon sun was beginning to fade behind the pines. Patty's parents would be coming to get her before suppertime. "We better hurry up," I said, glad she was going home. I didn't want to listen to her preaching at me about Buddy anymore. We reached the road, and pausing, I took off my sneaker, dumping out all the grove sand it had collected. A commotion coming from somewheres back down the road caused Patty and I both to turn. An old brown sedan and a couple pickup trucks were parked on the side of the road down by Senator Collier's house. All of a sudden three or four men came a running out of the Senator's property lickity split, like their lives' depended on it, and hopped in the back of one of the trucks. Tires spun and screeched across the asphalt as the three vehicles sped away towards the river road. I quickly put on my shoes and Patty and I, hopping on our bikes, began pedalling as fast as we could towards the Senator's.

Our mouths dropped wide open, but not a word passed between us as we approached the black wrought iron fence surrounding the property. Tied with twine to the iron posts was a big white sign blazoned with blood red words. I'm not sure how long we both just stood and stared, speechless, when a horsefly buzzed us and nearly flew in my gaping mouth. I jumped and Patty screamed grabbing my arm. We held on to one another and Patty began to read the words in front of us slowly and carefully, emphasizing each word, "No niggers in our schools." She repeated it, as if she was under some kind of trance. "What? Who would…"?

BZZZ! The horsefly buzzed us again and I caught its upward flight, "Oh-My-Gosh!" I said. There dangling from a low outstreched limb of an oak was the most gosh awful looking thing. Hanging there with a hangman's noose wrapped tightly round its neck was the likeness of a colored man shaped with straw and by the smell of it, black tar. Little prickly goosebumps ran up my arms. By now Patty had seen the hideous creation too.

"Would you take a look at that!" So that's what those men were up to and high tailing it out of here for. "You don't suppose they saw us do you? That wouldn't be good, not good at all. I mean men like that and all. Do you realize what they would have done to us if they had seen us?" Patty rambled on and on.

"We'd a known it if they'd seen us. Quit your frettin'," I told her.

"Why do you suppose they did this?" Patty asked.

"Well, it sure beats me. All I know is I'm getting the hell out of here before somebody thinks we did it." I said, lifting my kickstand and getting back on my bike, with Patty gasping and mumbling after me for saying the H word.

"It was a slip of the tongue," I grumbled, not really caring after what I'd just seen.

When we reached the Jackson place the Boyds were sitting in their car in the driveway talking to my Mom and Dad. We dropped the bikes on their sides and ran to the car, both of us talking at once trying to tell what had happened. Dad hushed us and said to slow down and speak one at a time. Patty let me do the talking, and I swear I never saw a group of grownups so quiet afterwards. All you could hear was Jack Jackson's bees buzzing off in the distance. Mrs. Boyd broke the silence.

"What on earth were you girls doing down there anyhow?"

"We were just taking a bike ride," Patty told her mother who was glaring at me. Like it was my fault or something.

"Well, the Senator is up to the State Capitol in Tallahassee this week," Dad said, "So I suppose we better call the Sheriff about this."

"You read about that sort of thing in bigger cities, but not in little towns like DeLeon," said Mom, shaking her head.

"Well, not every little town has their very own Senator, especially such a controversial one," Mr. Boyd said, "There'll be more trouble coming, I guarantee it, what with his stand on the schools and…"

"Paul!" Mrs. Boyd said looking from her husband and then to Patty and me.

"What's going on with the schools?" Patty asked.

"Nothing for you children to be concerned with," Mrs. Boyd said, telling Patty to come along. It seemed like every time things started getting exciting it was time for children to disappear or quit asking questions. The Boyds left and Dad went in to call the Sheriff. The only explanation I got was it had something to do with some people called KK or other that didn't like coloreds, and the Senator made them mad by voting in favor of the coloreds' rights. The whole thing made my head spin. Imagine adults pulling stunts like that.

Later when Buddy and Larry returned they were full of talk after seeing the Sheriff down by the Senator's.

"The Sheriff wanted to know if we'd seen anything," Buddy said. "But of course we hadn't," he went on.

Well of course they hadn't. They were too darn busy smoking cigarettes with the 'crazy' old colored man, I thought. But they didn't tell anyone about any of that.

After supper out on the porch I asked Bud if he had ever seen the crazy old man at the boathouse again after he and Larry had first seen him, and asked how they knew for sure he was crazy. I was hoping he'd break down and tell me his secret. Bud's eyebrows raised up, "Cally, don't you go messing around down there. You never know about those kind of stories, but usually where there's smoke there's fire."

"Patty Boyd's father told her that all colored men carry six-inch switchblades," I told him.

"Well, there you go. Just stay clear of the place. I wouldn't want you to end up fish food or gator bait," Bud said.

I didn't let on I knew his secret. Bud was growing up and spent more time on his own and with his friends than he used to. I didn't want him to be mad at me for discovering his secret place and maybe stay away more. He'd talk to me when he was ready. We used to talk a lot.

That night in bed I thought about the little colored man laughing and sitting on the dock with Bud and Larry. He looked harmless, almost grandfatherly. Shoot. Maybe I'd just go down there myself one day. I liked fishing and maybe he'd let me fish off his dock. I was glad he wasn't crazy or a killer.

CHAPTER FIVE

Bud came running in the front door, as a car pulled out the drive. His face was flushed with excitement, and his eyes sparkled. "Hi Cal," he said, tossing his schoolbooks on the recliner as he ran past me into the kitchen. "Mom, I got the job!" he said. I ran in to hear what had gotten him so all fired up.

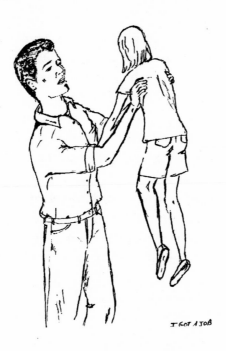

I GOT A JOB

"Job?" Mom looked confused.

"Cally girl," Bud said, picking me up in the air and swinging me around, "No more old blue motor scooter rides. From now on you'll ride in style when I get my car. After Mom, you'll get the first ride."

"Whoa, Buddy. What job, and what car?" Mom asked half smiling from his excitement.

"Larry dropped me off at Setzer's Grocery after school. They need another bagger and stockboy, and I got the job. Now I can get my license next week when I turn sixteen, and buy Jack Jackson's old gray Plymouth he keeps locked up in the shed out back. All I need is $100.00."

"And what does your Dad say about all this, or does he know the big plan yet?" Mom asked.

"Dad knows all about it. He and Mr. Jackson discussed it the other day," Bud explained, but not very well, because Mom looked suspicious. Bud, seeing the look too, added, "Well, that is, Mr. Jackson asked Dad if he didn't think it was high time I had something better to drive than that old blue scooter, and…"

"What did Dad say?" Mom said folding her arms across her.

Bud kind of looked away from Mom's questioning eyes and said, "Dad said that when Bud gets a job and can pay for the car we'll talk. So see the car's practically mine," he told her.

"We'll see," was all Mom said as Bud retreated to the living room.

I followed Mom as she walked into the living room behind Bud. She put her arms around his neck resting her head across his shoulder and whispered in his ear, "Congratulations on your job, I'm proud of you."

Bud smiled, hugging her arm. After mom went back in the kitchen I told Bud, "I don't mind riding with you on the old blue scooter. I really had a lot of fun. We haven't gone riding in a long time…"

Bud smiled, "Scooters are for kids, Cal. When I get my car we'll go riding and if you swear to keep it our little secret, I'll teach you how to drive out on some of these old back roads."

"I swear, Bud," I said grinning all over myself when Kate and Lynn came down the stairs.

"What was all the commotion about down here earlier, and what are you so smiley about," Kate asked, looking at me suspiciously.

"I'm smiling because…uh…Bud's got a job at Setzer's and he's going to buy Jack Jackson's old Plymouth," I told her.

"A car? Freedom at last. We can go into town on Saturdays and see our friends. I'll ride shotgun," said Kate.

"Why do you get to?" Lynn asked.

"Because, I'm next to the oldest," Kate announced proudly.

"Hold on, I haven't even got the car yet and ya'll are already arguing over it. Besides I promised Cally, she gets first ride, after Mom," he said with a wink. I smiled smugly at Kate.

"What's shotgun?" I asked.

"Oh brother," Kate rolled her eyes.

"That means you get to ride up front with me on the passenger side," Bud told me. I couldn't wait until my friends saw me riding in Bud's car, or maybe even driving it. They would be so jealous. I'd be so cool. Me and Bud. When I went with Bud he didn't treat me like a little kid, or get embarrassed when his friends saw me with him, like some of them did with their younger brothers and sisters.

Lynn turned on the television. Dick Clark's bandstand was on. "Oh, my gosh, Kate look, it's Frankie Avalon," Lynn squealed.

Never for the life of me could I figure out why older girls always squealed and screeched whenever they saw those rock and roll singers. I mean I liked Frankie, and 'Venus' was the first record I ever bought, but those girls on the television went crazy. They would pull their hair and cry and act like fools over those guys. Dad said they had the St. Vitas's Dance. I guessed with all their twitching and carrying on that about summed it up.

Somebody knocked at the door and before anyone could get to it, it opened and a voice said, "Anybody here?" It was Larry and Bill, Bud's friends. They walked on in.

Larry and Bill had been Bud's best friends since grade school. All of Kate's friends thought they were really cool. They each were so different looking, but handsome for teenage boys I guessed. Not exactly Cary Grant, but handsome for boys. Larry's hair was sun bleached and he had the dreamiest green eyes according to Lynn, and I couldn't disagree. Bill was just the opposite, tall, dark and muscle bound. He was on the football team. Bud was the youngest of the three, but would turn sixteen the day before Halloween. Even though Bud was my brother I had to admit he was the handsomest of the three with his dark hair and steel blue eyes. Kate said some of the girls in Bud's grade called him Elvis. Especially Bette Davis, not the movie star, but Kate said she thought she was. She was very mature for her age according to Kate and her friends. An early bloomer. Kate said she thought Bette D. was in love with Bud. Now that was the most ridiculous thing I ever heard tale of. Bud was only sixteen, almost. There was even an older woman, at least eighteen or nineteen chasing after Bud. That is until Mom put a stop to it. That woman kept calling, and one day even came over in her yellow convertible looking for Bud. Mom told Bud that girls like that were a little too bold for her taste and she didn't think it was a good idea to encourage her. I don't think she needed much encouraging, and I don't think Bud really minded the attention, but after that the girl quit calling him.

"We thought you had died or something," Kate told Bill who hadn't been over since we had moved.

"Well, you moved way out here in the boondocks," Bill teased her.

"See, what I tell ya'll?" Kate asked throwing her hands up.

"Don't mind Kate, our social butterfly. She hates it out here," Bud said.

Bill grabbed Kate up out of the chair, and reached over to turn up the television. "Come on Katie," Bill said. "Show me the bop. I've got to be in form for Bud's party Saturday night."

Bud was going to have a real boy-girl party on Halloween. Costumes and everything. I couldn't wait. Patty was going to stay over and spend the weekend. We could spy on them and watch that Bette Davis girl chase after Bud.

Kate pulled away from Bill, acting like she didn't want to dance. I wondered why she pretended to hate it so darn much. She had a big crush on him. She even wrote it in her diary. Patty and I read it. I told her, "Kate go on, you know you want to." She flashed an evil look, and I knew she would get me back later. Lynn was showing Larry how Carla and Tony, the dancers in the Bandstand spotlight dance did a move. Bud grabbed me up and started swinging me all over the place. "Come on half-pint, show them how it's done." They'd practice all the latest dances with us girls so they wouldn't look like fools at the school dances and parties like Bud's.

Bud went out to the kitchen to get some chips and pop. I watched Larry and Lynn as she held onto his finger and he raised his arm up over her head, spinning her in circles. I'd had the biggest crush on Larry ever since I could remember. Watching him I thought about a couple summers ago and softly touched my cheek remembering THE KISS.

Larry and Bud were sitting out on the breezeway putting together a model car. They were talking about the 'Firecracker 250' race at Daytona on the Fourth of July. Larry had gone with his Dad and uncle. Larry told Bud, the excitement in his voice racing, "Fireball Roberts' car was so cool. Shit he passed all those other guys like they were sitting still. When he came into that final lap I thought sure he'd never make it across the finish. But, sure enough, he came flying across, his engine smoking like a damn house afire. My Daddy was sweatin' it out pretty bad. He bet a bunch on the Robert's car."

"Yeah, I watched it on T.V. It was a helluva race. Wish I'd been there," Bud said. Bud and Larry liked to swear a lot when they were together. I decided they thought it was the cool thing to do. So, I knew how I would impress Larry. I got my blackboard out and I set it up so the boys could get a good look. Sounding out what seemed to be one of Larry's favorite words; I wrote in big white chalk letters across the black slate, S-H-I-T. Finally, after I had cleared my throat so much it was raw, and got their attention, I pretended to doodle on the board, my back to them. I could hear them laughing and then all at once they got real quiet. I thought I'd jump clean out of my skin when I heard my Mother's angry voice filling the breezeway, "Cally Cummins, what do you think you're doing?" My face got red hot and little beads of sweat were all over my upper lip. There was no denying this. There it was in black and white. Punishment came swift. I could see Bud grimace and squint his eyes knowing what was in store. He'd been there a few years back. To this day, I swear I can't even look at a bar of Lifebouy Soap. But it was worth it. Later, when I sat all alone in front of a clean slate, feeling sorry for myself, Larry snuck up behind me and gave me a tender kiss on my cheek. Then he just walked away. I knew he felt sorry for me, but I didn't care why he done it, just that he had.

Bill's voice broke my daydream. "Hey Bud, someone's coming up your drive."

Bud came in and looked through the window. "It's Jack Jackson coming to check on his bees. Come on, I'll see if he'll let us look at the car," Bud said. The boys took off out the back of the house. I followed after them, leaving Lynn and Kate to listen to Dick Clark count off the top ten.

Jack Jackson pulled the old car out of the shed, and each boy took his turn sitting behind the wheel. Then they opened the hood and stared at the pile of wires and metal talking, about spark plugs and carburetors. "Hot damn, that's one cherry piece of machinery. If Bud doesn't buy it I will," Bill said.

"I got my job at Setzer's today, Mr. Jackson," Bud said. "I turn sixteen next weekend and as soon as I get my license I'm gonna buy her if it's okay with you."

"As long as your Dad says you can, Buddy Boy, it's yours," Jack Jackson told Bud and added, "So you turn sixteen next weekend?"

"Yes sir," Bud said smiling. "Bud's having a party Halloween night, a real boy/girl costume party," I told Jack Jackson.

"Halloween night, huh? Well, this here is a good area to have a Halloween Party. Folks say there's a lot of ghosts come out around these parts on All Hallows Eve. Get them young gals all scared and they won't turn you loose," Jack Jackson laughed.

"Ghosts, come on, you're not serious," Larry said.

"Oh I'm serious, dead serious," the big man told Larry stone-faced.

He had my attention, and from the looks of it the boys' too.

Jack Jackson continued, "Years ago, when these here homes along this road were brand spankin' new, they were plum full of rich grove owners. Hell, some of these houses are a hundred years old or more. There was a banker and a state senator too. Senator Collier's family still lives in the home his granddaddy built. It passed on down through the generations to him. Most of these groves were much bigger than they are now.

Bountiful, full of fruit and lush. The owners hired colored folks to work the groves. Slaves in the beginning, but after those days were gone, most of the colored families stayed on and worked the groves for a living. They were treated well by the earlier owners, and being as that was all they knew, they stayed. They lived in old shanty's built on the properties, like the family of old Isaac down at the boathouse; I believe you two boys are acquainted with Isaac," he said looking at Larry and Bud. "I seen your old blue scooter down there quite a lot," he explained. Bud looked at me and I just smiled at him. "Saw you and that little red-headed friend of yours down there one day too Cally; peeking through the windows," Jack Jackson informed me. Bud smiled this time shaking his head. "Anyways, old Isaac's grandmother worked for the Senator's family. A cook I believe. She's buried down there at the old colored cemetery around the bend near the boathouse. Isaac is sort of the self-proclaimed caretaker of the rundown cemetery. A lot of bad things happened to some of those poor coloreds around the days when nightriders, or the Klan as you might know them today, were big in these parts. They would catch them off in the dark of night and frighten them half to death. The story goes that the nightriders hung a couple of colored boys down by the old River House Hotel. It was deserted for years, but I hear tell it's some kind of Hunt Club now. But, they say it's haunted. They say this whole area is. The spirits of those two poor boys and all the rest of the colored folks buried in that cemetery come out on Halloween night to whoop it up and scare white folks," Jack Jackson finished. All eyes were on him, and not a sound, except our breath could be heard.

"Funny Isaac never talks about any of that stuff," Bud said, breaking the silence.

"Colored folks are pretty superstitious about the dead and the things of the spirit world. He's probably scared to talk about it. But you ask him if the remains of his dearly departed grandmother ain't in that cemetery. He'll tell you," Jack Jackson said.

"Where's Isaac's family at, his parents and all?" Bud asked.

"They moved away, over around Ocala I heard, when Isaac was a young man. One real bad winter, the smudge pots couldn't keep up, and some of the groves got froze out. They had to be replanted. It takes a long time to produce fruit again. The rest of his family moved on, but Isaac stayed. Isaac got a job at the boathouse, as a maintenance man. The owner let him live in the room in the back. He's got a stove and a bed and all he needs in there. He's lived there for years. I'd say his parents are probably real old if not gone by now. I figure Isaac is close to sixty himself."

I decided to go back into the house and leave Bud and the boys to talk about ghosts and cars and old colored men.

I didn't sleep too well that night after all that ghost talk. Jack Jackson's words filled my mind. I wondered if there were any ghosts hanging around the Jackson house. If there were they probably wouldn't be too happy about Patty and me stealing those tangelos from the Anderson grove where they worked so hard, even if it was an honest mistake. So I said my prayers and threw in a few good words about them oranges. "Lord, they were mighty good tangelos. Thank them colored folks up there for growing such good fruit for me to taste. I promise I'll never take another, Amen." An old owl hooted off in the distance, and I covered my head.

"Cally, quit mumbling and wiggling around, and go to sleep," Lynn said sleepily.

CHAPTER SIX

Friday, October 30, finally came. Bud's birthday. Patty came home with me after school. At dinner, Bud showed off his new driver's license. Dad gave in about the car after hearing about Bud's job. Bud blew out the candles on his German Chocolate cake; that was his favorite. We always got our favorite meal plus whatever kind of cake for our birthdays. I always wanted T-bone steak. Bud chose Mom's homemade cabbage rolls. After cake Bud went out with Larry and Bill to celebrate getting his license. Everyone else headed for the living room to watch "Sea Hunt". Patty and I decided we would go upstairs and find some of Bud's comics to read. He had just about all the *Superman* and *Archie* comics there ever were.

"Just get the comics and don't stay in your brother's room, Cally. You know he doesn't like anyone messing with his things," Mom said as Patty and I headed up the stairs. "Cally?" she repeated.

"Okay, Mom," I answered. Bud had a lot of really cool things in his room. On his desk was an Indian tipi with his collection of real arrow heads inside. There were lots of model cars on shelves and an album with baseball cards. He had Mickey Mantle, Roger Maris and Whitey Ford. They were my favorites.

I opened his night stand by his bed and started digging through the comics. Pulling out his latest *Archie*, I said, "I hope I look just like Betty when I grow up," looking at the cover. Digging further down there was a thick one near the bottom. "What's this one?" I said, pulling it out. "Holy smoke," was all I could say as one of the pages came tumbling out from its center.

I Buds Room

"Would you get a look at that," Patty said. "Cally Cummins, your brother Bud looks at girly magazines," she said covering her mouth with her hand.

"Says here her name is Lydia, and she's a librarian?" I said reading the words in the little box beside Lydia's full length picture.

"I doubt she's ever read a book, let alone worked in a library," Patty said.

"Patty, do you suppose we'll look like that someday?" "I don't know, I don't think I've ever seen anybody that looks quite like that," she said.

"Is that what they mean when they say somebody has bloomed? If it is I can't wait 'til I bloom," Patty snickered.

"Yeah, forget Betty, I want to look like that," I decided.

"Cally, are you still in Bud's room?" Mom hollered up the stairs. I hurried up and folded Lydia up and stuck her back in the magazine and shoved it back in the drawer. We turned out the light and hurried downstairs. "We changed our minds, we're going to watch *Sea Hunt*," I said.

Later, Patty said Bud would probably go to hell for reading those kind of magazines. I didn't know about that, but I knew there would be hell to pay if Mom or Dad found out. So I told Patty to swear to never tell anyone. She said she wasn't allowed to swear, but not to worry.

The next day, while Bud was working at Setzer's, and Dad was at work, me, Patty, Mom and my sisters cleaned and got the house ready for the party. We decorated the big glassed in part of the wrap-around porch where Bud wanted to have the party, with cob webs of cotton gauze and pumpkins from Jack Jackson's patch. On the rest of the open porch we put the smaller cut out pumpkins each with a candle in it to make jack o'lanterns. Mom and Kate supervised Lynn, Patty and me while we made popcorn balls and candy apples. Kate sighed, "I almost wish Lynn and I weren't going to the party at the Armory. Bud's party will be so much fun."

"Bud said Patty and I can hang around for a while until we go trick-or-treating," I reminded Mom.

"Well, just make sure you don't annoy Bud and his friends. He's real nervous about this party," Mom cautioned.

"Bud doesn't mind me hanging around his friends," I said.

"This is a little different Cally," Mom said. "There'll be girls coming and teenage boys get nervous as long tailed cats in a room full of rocking chairs when teenage girls are around. Little sisters can make it worse, especially if they get too nosy," she said.

"I hear you, Mom. Patty and I have big plans anyway, right?" I said, poking Patty. She nodded.

"I'm not too sure I like the sounds of that either, but I have too much else to worry about today," Mom said pouring a batch of popcorn into the creamy caramel sauce.

Bud came home with Dad after work. He was a nervous wreck, just like Mom warned he would be. He looked around at the decorations and hugged Mom, then ran upstairs to shower. Out in the kitchen Dad told Mom, "I swear that boy talked my ear off all the way home."

"He's just nervous about the party. He wants everything to be right," Mom told Dad.

"He was asking me about girls and I gave him a refresher talk on the birds and bees," Dad said, tickling Mom on her side.

She saw that I had been standing there and her face blushed. "We better eat dinner now so everyone can get their costumes on," she said giving Dad a look. He winked at her and she blushed again.

After supper Patty and I got out our costumes. She was Dracula. Kate took Mom's black eyebrow pencil and colored Patty's bangs. "Your cape can cover the rest of your head, but Dracula can't go around with red bangs," Kate said rubbing in the pencil. I was a black cat. Mom had sewn a cotton stuffed tail to my tights and made a black cap with pointed ears for my head. After we were ready we went downstairs to get out of Kate and Lynn's way. Bud was in the living room pacing around.

"Bud, do you believe that story Jack Jackson told us about the colored cemetery?" I asked.

Bud looked menacing as he gave a devilish smile. He wrapped his red cape from his devil's costume around Patty and whispered in her ear, "Yes, and I hear they all were buried with their six-inch switchblades." He moved his finger across her throat.

Kate and Lynn came bouncing down the stairs. Bud turned loose of Patty. Lynn was dressed as a hobo, wearing a pair of Bud's old pants she had sewed patches on. She wore an old flannel shirt with suspenders to hold up the too large pants. Her curly auburn hair was tamed into two braids that fell down her back. One of Dad's hats sat on top of her head.

Kate had smudged eyebrow pencil all over Lynn's face to look like dirt. Bud laughed as Kate came in behind Lynn. "I thought you were supposed to be the wicked witch of the East," he told her.

"She decided to be Glenda, the good witch, because if she looks uglier than sin, Billy Carson won't dance with her," Lynn said one of Dad's Havanas bobbing up and down from her lips as she talked. Kate shoved her.

Car lights shown in the window. "There's the Thompson's," Lynn said, "Come on, Katie Good Witch, grab your broom and let's fly." Lynn swung her baton over her shoulder, narrowly missing the table lamp with her handkerchief bundle tied to the end of the baton. Hugging Mom and Dad at the door, they headed to the Armory with the Thompsons.

It was about an hour before Bud's guests were due to come so he, Patty and I moved the Hi-Fi through the french doors of the living room onto the glassed in porch. Bud got all his forty-fives, and the ones he borrowed and put them in stacks.

"Are you going to play any games, Bud?" I asked. "Maybe," he answered, still stacking records. "What kind?" I asked, Patty and I exchanging knowing smiles.

"None of your business; you'll be out of here by then anyways," Bud said getting agitated.

"I knew it! You're going to play kissing games with that Bette Davis girl. I'll bet Liz is coming with Larry too. Mom and Dad won't like it," I warned him.

"Mom and Dad will be watching *Mike Hammer* just like every Saturday night, and you and Dracula here will be out terrorizing the neighborhood by then. Cally, if you say a word I swear I'll deny it and tell Mom you can't come to my party at all," Bud said, getting more nervous.

"Relax, your secret's safe with us, you devil you," I said, grabbing Patty's arm, pulling her with me towards the kitchen to get a popcorn ball.

Pretty soon the guests started to arrive while Jerry Lee Lewis' "Great Balls of Fire" pounded out of the Hi-Fi. Patty and I peaked through the curtains on the french doors watching all the ghosts and vampires trouping in. One guy had a fake knife stuck to his head with a bunch of really sick looking red stuff around it.

"Good gosh!" I said, nudging Patty to look at the leopard girl coming through the door. She had long dark auburn hair that matched the spots on her leopard costume, which only covered one shoulder, the costume's other side bared her other shoulder and a whole lot more. She wore tights and high spiked heels. She walked right up to Bud and his eyes were glued to her like Jack Jackson's honey. "That's her, that's Bette Davis," I said.

"She's gorgeous, just like one those girls in Bud's magazine," Patty said.

"Yeah, I wonder if she's going to be a librarian," I said. We were giggling when Dad came up and told us, "In or out girls, don't stand in the doorway, or you'll get your heads knocked off if one of those yahoos comes through here."

We went on the porch and all the girls made over us, saying things like, "Oh, Bud, aren't they adorable," and Oh, Bud this and Oh, Bud that, batting their eyes. They acted almost as goofy as the boys did around the opposite sex.

Bill came up and wanted to know what kind of mischief we were planning on later. We both just gave him shrugged shoulders and innocent grins. "That's what I thought," he said handing me, a bar of soap. It wasn't Lifebouy. "Don't do too much damage," he said, and "Watch out for those ghosts when you get down by the cemetery. Especially watch out for their eyes. That's all you'll see at first you know. When somebody dies all that's left after their spirits leave are glowing eyeballs."

"Oh, you're so full of bull," I told him.

"We'll see," he laughed an evil laugh. Turning away a pair of sunglasses sat on the back of his head that flashed little eyeballs in their plastic lenses.

"Very funny," I said. After a while Mom came out and told Patty and me it was time to go trick-or-treating before it got too late.

"You girls be back here no later than 9:30 you hear, and you carry this with you, Cally," she said, handing me a flashlight. She and Dad turned on the television as we went out the front door.

"Come on around here first," I told Patty running around the side of the house to the glassed in porch. As we peeked in, all the boys were sitting down in a big circle. One guy put the needle on the record and started the music, while another flipped the lights off. The music stopped. The lights flicked back on and there was all kinds of commotion as all the girls pushed and tripped to stop in front of a certain boy. Then all a sudden the boy grabbed them and kissed them.

"We never played musical chairs like that," Patty said. We watched a couple more rounds laughing so hard we had to sit down as Bette nearly broke her neck in her high heels trying to move the other girls on by Bud.

"We better get going," I said. So Patty and I walked across the yard towards the Anderson's. The Andersons were old people and they made us come in so they could see us and ooh and ahh over us. We really didn't mind though because we wanted to see the inside of the big two-story colonial. It was beautiful inside. The Anderson house had black marble floors and a red carpeted stairway that wound clean up to the second floor. Mom and Dad said Mr. Anderson was retired from some place called Wall St. The Andersons said how scared we made them, then gave us some cider from a fancy glass punch bowl and two donuts apiece off a silver tray.

House after house we filled our Setzer Grocery bags chock full of candy, apples and we even got a dime from the Westhoffs. Mr. Westhoff was the President of the National Bank in downtown DeLeon. Patty said, "He probably stole them dimes," because it was his bank and he could do whatever he wanted with the money.

By the time we reached the turn in the road, down by the boathouse, we couldn't put anymore in our bags. We only soaped one house because they wouldn't come to the door. We decided to find a spot to sort through and eat some of the candy so we could get some more. Being as we didn't have to worry about any crazy colored man getting us, namely old Isaac, we sat down on the wooden fence rails in front of the boathouse to do our sorting. The moon was high above the pine trees and it scattered streams of milky white light along the paved road and into the woods. We sat there for a few moments with the only sound interrupting the night's quiet being the crumpling of candy wrappers, I told Patty, "I've got some room in here now."

"Me too," she said. We both shook our bags so the remaining candy packed down in the bottom.

"Let's go on down to the three houses past the cemetery, then we'll be done," I suggested.

"I think I've got plenty here. My Mom said I've got soft teeth and too much candy will rot them," Patty said.

"That's the biggest bunch of gosh darn boloney Patty Boyd. You're just afraid to go by the cemetery because of that stuff I told you Jack Jackson said," I told her.

"Don't say gosh darn, and I'm not afraid. I just don't need anymore candy," she said.

"Now why can't I say gosh darn, gosh darn, gosh darn it all?" I said taunting her.

"It's the same as saying the Lord's name in vain that's why," she answered.

"Is not. Gosh darn just means gosh darn. I didn't say the Lord's name, I never do, gosh darn it anyways," I said.

"Something bad is going to happen if you keep saying it," Patty warned.

"Well, I'm going on around the bend, so either come on with me or go on back to the house by yourself," I said so gosh darn tired of her preaching at me. Secretly I was a little scared too, but Lynn said ghosts didn't come out until after midnight anyways.

We started by the cemetery. Patty grabbed my arm. She was shaking fearfully.

"Now what's the matter," I asked.

"I just saw eyeballs flashing across the way," she said.

"Where?" I asked. Patty pointed at two small lights bouncing around on the far side of the cemetery. I turned off my flashlight and hid behind an old stone pillar, motioning for Patty to follow. "That's not eyeballs," I whispered, "It's somebody else with flashlights."

All of a sudden Patty gasped in a big deep breath and when I looked over at her, her cheeks were pouched out like a chipmunk's, full of air. She was holding her breath. "What in the Sam Hill do you think your doing?" I asked her.

Out came a breath in a big gush, and she quickly said, "You're supposed to hold your breath when you go by a cemetery. That way the spirits can't get in and suck out your soul." Then she took another big gulp of air.

"If you keep doin' that you're going to pass out and they'll get you for sure," I said.

There was a thumping and sliding sound like someone digging a shovel into the ground. A girl's muffled laughter and a boy's voice came from the same direction. In a loud whisper the boy said, "Shut up, do you want to wake the dead?" More laughter. Patty and I left our candy by the post and crawled around the back end of the cemetery, post to post to get a little closer. Their speech was slurred and they kept shushing each other and laughing. They appeared to be two boys and a girl about Bud's age. The three of them were passing a long necked bottle back and forth, each taking a swig from it as the boys dug the ground up. After some time the shovel hit something with a thud, and the one boy with the shovel started digging faster, scraping against whatever the shovel had hit. Then he threw down the shovel and both boys crawled down in the hole.

"They're digging up some old colored person's grave," Patty whispered, her voice quivering.

"I can see that, but what on earth for," I whispered back. We were both shaking so hard we held onto each other tight. Suddenly the boys crawled out of the hole and the taller one held something in his hands. He turned to show the girl and she let out with an awful screech and the other boy put his hand over her mouth. "Shut up Mary Jo," he told her.

"Let's get out of here," the other boy said. Just then some branches crunched behind an oak tree near where Patty and I stood when we first saw the flashlights. It was the old colored man Isaac. I didn't think he had seen us, so we sat perfectly still as the kids started up their car. Headlights off, they drove away past the oak tree where Isaac stood hidden watching the car pass.

"We've got to get out of here. I told you something bad would happen," Patty said.

"We can't go anywhere until Isaac leaves," I said, "We just watched a bunch of graverobbers. If we get caught here the police will take us down and make us tell what we know, and then the robbers will come find us and Lord knows what they'll do to us." We both just sat in silence and watched Isaac walk across the graveyard to the opened grave. We crawled on our hands and knees to the edge of the cemetery and got up and ran as fast as we could. About half way back home I realized we forgot our bags of candy. "Oh shoot, gosh darn it all Patty we forgot our candy," I said stopping in my tracks.

"Forget about it Cally, we'll get it tomorrow," Patty said.

"Yeah, after the ants eat their fill," I said disgusted, but not about to go back there now.

By the time we got back to the house Patty's Cinderella watch said it was ten 'til ten. Bud's party was still going strong and we snuck up on the porch and into the party. Nobody seemed to notice, they were dancing close and Larry and Liz were swapping spit. I gave a little sigh and we went into the living room. Mom and Dad were both asleep in their chairs. Dad was snoring in competition with the CBS test pattern filling the television screen.

Looking down at our dirty knees and hands we quietly slipped up the stairs to clean up and hop into to bed before we were noticed.

CHAPTER SEVEN

"Ouch," I said. Something was jabbing me in the side. There it went again. "What the heck," I said. I tried to close my eyes tight against the morning light that was prying them open.

"Cally," Patty's voice broke the quiet.

"Ouch," there it went again. It was Patty jabbing me awake.

"Cally, wake up. Listen. What's that noise?" Patty said.

Rrroar!

"Huh?" It was taking me some time to figure out where I was. I had been dreaming about digging up a garden. Everytime I dug something up it was an empty candy wrapper. The candy eaten by Lord only knows what.

Rrroar!

"Cally?"

"Oh, for crying out loud," I said realizing what it was that had her all stirred up, "It's the lions down at the circus place. You remember? The circus trucks we saw?" I rolled over and covered my eyes. Then it hit me. I was wide awake now. "Candy. Oh my gosh," I said and turned to look at Patty. She looked so funny. The black eyebrow pencil from her hair was all over her forehead and her bangs were all stuck together poking out like a horn from the top of her head.

"What's so funny?" she said.

"Look in the mirror on the bureau," I said crawling out of bed and grabbing my clothes off the chair. "Let's get dressed and go down and get our candy before everybody wakes up," I said.

"I think you're a little late on that one Cally. Can't you just taste the bacon cooking? That's what woke me," Patty said.

My stomach growled. "It does smell pretty good doesn't it? Let's go wash up and eat, then we'll go find our candy before your mom and dad come to get you for church," I said.

We peeked in Kate's room and she and Lynn were dead to the world. Little snores came from under the sheets.

Down in the kitchen Dad was sitting at the table reading the Sunday paper while Mom turned eggs on the griddle. "Good morning!" I said, my mouth set for salty bacon and cheese grits.

"How's our two goblins doing this morning?" Mom said, "You two must have been all tuckered out when you got home last night. You were sound asleep when we went up to check on you."

"By the looks of those two Setzer bags you two must have made a pretty good haul last night," Dad said sticking his head out from behind the paper. Patty and I looked at one another, then back at Dad. "You're lucky you still have anything left leaving them on the porch like that. I'm surprised the Anderson's Setter didn't make off with it all," Dad said as Patty and I looked dumbfounded at one another again. Dad put the paper down. "What's the matter with you two, your eyes are bulged out like a couple bull frogs. Oh, I get it. Don't worry, I brought them in with the paper. I ate someone's Milky Way, but that's all. I swear! You've got enough there to last until Easter," Dad said going back to the paper.

"Where did you put the bags, Dad?" I asked.

"They're on the coffee table," he said pointing a long finger over the top of the paper towards the living room.

Patty and I nearly tripped over one another to get in the other room. "Don't go eating any candy now. I've just about got breakfast ready for you," Mom said.

I sat down on the couch staring at the two bags. Patty was checking hers for bugs. "Who do you suppose brought these here, Cally?" Patty said.

"Who do you think?" I said, "It must have been Isaac." A cold chill ran up my back.

"He was here? Last night?" Patty asked. "I wonder why he didn't keep it all for himself. He must be a pretty nice guy," Patty said, shoving a Tootsie Roll in her mouth.

"Yeah, let's hope he's nice enough not to tell Bud and Larry. They find out we were down at that cemetery last night and saw all that went on, I'm in big trouble. You know how it is. Your parents find out one thing, then next thing you know there's a zillion questions and pretty soon they know we were late and I'm grounded," I said.

"Breakfast," Mom called. "Don't mention anything about last night," I told Patty. By the time Patty and I were finished with breakfast, Lynn, Kate and Bud had decided to join the living. Passing them in the hallway Bud was the last to troupe by. Stepping in front of me he whispered, "A little late getting back last night weren't you Cal?"

"How would you know? Your eyes were stuck to Jane of the Jungle when we came in," I told him.

"I keep my eye out for my little sister," he said. Lowering my eyes I asked, "You gonna tell?" Bud smiled, "Save me a Three Musketeers and I'll think about it," and he went in the kitchen.

"Bud is so neat," Patty said, "Paul would tell on me in a minute."

Paul Boyd was a big jerk, I thought. Patty and I went upstairs to get into our Sunday clothes. We were just in time for her parents to pick her up. Mom and Dad hurried the sleepy heads through breakfast and upstairs to get ready so we wouldn't be late to the Methodist church.

Before services the high school kids were gathered around in front of the church by the steps whispering and acting real peculiar, even for them. Clara Webb seemed to be at the center of attention. She was the second biggest gossip in town. Her Mom was the first. Mom said that Clara and her Mother were worse than any two old women when it came to telling tales. They knew what happened before anybody in town. Sometimes before the people it was supposed to have happened to. Whatever she was saying provoked more "Lords" and "Jesus Christs" from the crowd than we ever had heard said in church. Somewhere from the middle of the crowd a girl said real surprised like, "Mary Jo?" She was hushed quiet by Clara.

"Mary Jo," I said to myself. "Where in Sam Hill had I heard that…Oh good gosh!" I said out loud looking to see if anyone had heard. If I could just sneak up a little closer so as to hear Clara's big mouth.

I jumped a foot when Lynn grabbed hold of my arm saying "Come on Cally, we'll be late for church."

"You scared the daylights out of me. Don't ever go sneakin' up on me like that," I said. It figured, just when things were getting interesting.

All during church I kept trying to figure out who the mysterious Mary Jo might be. She's someone those big kids know, so she'd probably be in Bud's yearbook. I decided first chance I got I'd check it out.

CHAPTERER EIGHT

Mom fixed us a quick lunch after church so she and Dad could go work at the new house. Dad told Bud he could go fishing with Larry and Bill being as he worked after school everyday that week.

For the first of November the days were pretty mild. It had been cool enough in the early mornings to keep the fruit sweet but not too cool so as to keep the flowers from blooming. Jack Jackson had said the other day his bees were having a good fall. "First freeze and that'll be it until Spring," He said. Kate and Bud waited on the fishermen from the front porch. Lynn was up in our room doing her homework so she could watch Walt Disney later. Now was as good a time as any to go up to Bud's room to check out his yearbook for Mary Jo. It didn't take long to find what I was looking for. Fortunately for me the Halloween moon had been just light enough to frame the small round face and see the golden hair of the girl, Mary Jo. I read the caption under the small girl jumping high off the football field. Mary Jo Harris, Varsity Cheerleader, Senior. That's it. That's where I'd seen her before. We had gone to the Homecoming game between DeLeon and Chambley. A bar of soap, of all things, was all a kid needed to get in. I loved to watch the cheerleaders. I had decided that's what I was going to do when I got in high school. Mary Jo was the prettiest. She was crowned Homecoming Queen at half-time. The other girls weren't near as pretty in their fancy gowns as she was in her cheerleading outfit. For the life of me I couldn't figure out what a girl like that was doing in the cemetery that night with those boys.

I heard a car and slammed the book shut putting it back on the shelf. Once downstairs I started to open the front door, but hesitated before going out. It was Larry and Bill. Bill was asking Bud if he heard the latest about Mary Jo Harris, and some boys named Sam and Tony.

"Yeah," Bud said, "At church today Clara Webb was saying the three of them came into the U. D. last night flashing somebody's skull around in a box."

Kate groaned and acted all spazzed out and said, "Why on earth would they take a dead person's skull to the University Drive-In? A hamburger joint? I'll bet that was appetizing."

"Squeaky Arnold said the three were drunk as skunks when they got there," Bill said.

"Probably just a cow's head," Larry laughed.

"No man, Clara said it was a real human head," Bud argued.

"That's sick," Larry said, and I quietly agreed, little goosebumps poppin' up on my arms.

"Where'd they get it if it was real?" asked Kate. I closed the door. If I went out there it would be too tempting to tell them what I knew.

The boys left to go fishing, and I'll be darned if they weren't still buzzing about that skull when they got back. Frankly, I was getting real tired hearing about that thing. My skinned crawled everytime I thought about that night. That head had to be what that boy poked in front of Mary Jo's face to make her scream like she did.

CHAPTER NINE

Monday, and it was business as usual at Jefferson Davis. Miss Rowell gave us a surprise math test and Hal Peterson and Tommy Roberts got caught cheating. That wasn't anything new. The two of them must have stayed up nights just trying to figure new ways to cheat. This time Tommy excused himself to the bathroom, and when he got back Hal raised his hand to go. Miss Rowell told Hal in a minute and sent Bobby Harper down to get Principal Stone. Principal Stone came and left, but when he came back in again with a wad of toilet paper with some scribbling all over it Tommy Roberts eyes filled with tears, and he started balling like a baby. Hal called him a name I'd never even heard before and Mr. Stone took them both down to the office. Ordinarily that story would have been pretty entertaining when I got home. But, before I got a chance to tell it, Bud came in so excited he appeared like he was about to bust.

"How come you're not at work?" Mom asked before he got a chance to talk.

"Setzer's only needed me for an hour today, so Larry brought me home," Bud said. "Wait 'til I tell you what happened at school today. What a day," he said grabbing one of the homemade rolls Mom was basting with butter after taking them from the oven. "I could smell these before I got in the door Mom," he said as he poured a glass of milk to go with the roll.

"So tell us what happened," Mom said impatiently.

Bud began, "Just before second period, Mary Jo Harris, Tony Maretti and Sam Bernstein were called down to the office over the P.A. system. Apparently the cops were waiting down there and escorted Tony to his locker and made him open it up. When he opened it there was a box inside with a skull in it. It must have been the one Clara Webb said the three of them had Halloween night up at the U.D."

I caught Mom's mortified grimace. "Anyway," Bud went on, "The cops took them away in their squad car and I guess to the jail. The Homecoming Queen, the President of the senior class and Sam Bernstein, whose Mom and Dad own the biggest store in DeLeon. They say Tony might be expelled."

"Mary Jo Harris?" Mom asked surprised. "You mean that cute little gal Robbie Olsen at church used to go with? Why, his Mother is in my church circle, and she was always saying what a sweet girl Mary Jo was. What a shame," Mom said shaking her head.

"Sam Bernstein and Maretti are pretty wild Mom. Both their parents are loaded. Those two get whatever they want. Sam just got a brand new MG for his birthday this year," Bud said.

"More money than brains," Mom said. She just kept shaking her head as Buddy talked.

"According to Clara, Mary Jo's been seeing Sam without her Mamma and Daddy's permission," Bud told her.

"Well, I bet they know it now. Goodness, I don't know what's the matter with some children; keeping secrets and sneaking around like that," Mom said.

I choked on my roll. "Time to do my homework or something," I said, high tailing it out of the kitchen.

Later, Mom came in the living room. "I thought you said earlier you were going to do your homework," she said.

"I didn't have much," I told her. She sat down to watch 'Little Rascals' on The Uncle Walt Show with me while supper finished in the oven.

Pretty soon Dad came in from work carrying the evening paper with him. "Would you look at this," he said, throwing the paper on the coffee table. "Right down the road. Right under our noses. What's the matter with kids these days?" he said.

Here we go again I thought. Mom looked at the big black letters across the front of the paper, "'Three Area Teens Vandalize Cemetery'. That must be the kids Bud came home all fired up about after school. I guess there was big trouble at the high school about it."

"Darn, I figured there'd be pictures," I said skimming the front page and looking inside. Dad explained they couldn't put kids pictures or names in the paper if they broke the law. Something or other about getting sued. "Shoot! They could have at least put a picture of the skull in," I said.

"Says there that the caretaker, a colored fella by the name of Isaac Washington, saw them leaving the scene and gave the license plate number of the one kid's car," Dad said.

Mom had taken the paper from me and was busy reading the article. "Oh my goodness. That's horrible. Says it was the grave of a colored boy supposedly hung by the Klan years ago."

Jack Jackson's story was true I said to myself.

"Little hoodlums," Dad was ranting now, "If that was one of my kids they wouldn't sit for a month."

At supper Dad was still pretty upset about the cemetery thing, but he'd moved on to something else that had him going now, concerning our neighbor, Senator Collier.

"The senator is sure making a lot of the wrong people mad," Dad told Mom. "That incident last month was just the beginning. Says here there's been some threats made on him if he pursues this integration thing with the schools," Dad said.

"What's all the fuss about?" I asked.

"It means colored kids will come to school with us," Lynn said, "Mr. Thompson said he'll pull Linda out of school if it happens, and send her to a private school."

"How come Senator Collier wants to make them come to our schools? I'll bet they won't want to. I hear the colored school has a swimming pool. We don't. Hey, maybe we'll get to go to theirs," I said.

Bud laughed and Dad gave him that look. Bud shut up real quick.

"Too bad adults don't see life as simply as our children do," Dad smiled at Mom.

"Well, what's the matter with colored folks?" I asked. "They got something wrong with them? Downtown they have their own water fountains and toilets in McCrory's, and the store makes them all sit over in the corner at the soda fountain. There's a big old sign posted when you go in that says "Colored Section." One time the white water fountain was busted in the back of the store, but I didn't drink out of the colored's 'cause Patty said I might get some disease or something."

Looking across the table Bud and Kate were shaking and turning so red-faced with laughter I thought they'd burst for sure. I could feel Lynn fidgeting around beside me.

"What's so darn funny," I asked glaring at Kate and Bud.

Bud kicked me from under the table.

"Bud, Kate that's about enough," Dad said. They both hung their heads like they were studying their plates of food, but they still were shaking.

Dad looked at me with his now soft blue eyes and said, a smile on his lips, "There's nothing wrong with being colored Cally. They're the same as you or me. There's good and bad in all colors. It's just that there are always folks out there who dislike or even hates others because they're different. I guess they're afraid of something. I don't know. Sometimes this world doesn't make a whole lot of sense.

"Well, I don't know why there's such a ruckus. Shoot, if colored people are all as nice as that fella' Mr. Washington then I say take down the signs and leave them be?" I said.

"How do you know Mr. Washington?" Dad asked putting his fork down.

"Oh… I don't know him…, but Bud says he's a real nice man," I said feeling another kick from under the table.

Dad picked his fork back up and commenced to stab a piece of meat and said, "All the ruckus is about something else called segregation, Cally. Laws say colored people can't mix in with white people."

"Ain't this supposed to be a free country?" I asked.

"Isn't this supposed to be a free country Cally," Dad smiled. After my correction in grammar he went on, "That's why Senator Collier and others like him are trying to change things. But, just because you change the rules and take down signs doesn't mean you can change people. That takes time. Things could get real ugly," Dad said.

Bud and Kate weren't laughing anymore. It was almost nine o'clock and we were watching Red Skeleton when somebody knocked at the door. When Mom opened it Larry and Bill nearly fell in. They were all in a tizzy. Their faces were wild with excitement and both of them were trying to talk at once.

Finally, Larry blurted out, "Mrs. Cummins, you won't believe what we just saw. Fire engines, cops and people all over."

"Where?" Mom said her voice startled.

Bill piped in, "In town! DeLeon. I think it's the Klan. A big cross is burning in front of Mary Jo Harris' house. We saw Bill Watson the cop that's always patrolling the U.D., so we stopped and asked what was going on. He said that the Klan lit up crosses in each of the kids' yards that dug up that colored boy Halloween night."

"Will, are you listening to all this?" Momma turned to Daddy, "Why on earth would the Klan burn crosses in white kid's yards for?" Dad was already on his way to the door.

"I don't know," Larry said, "But the sheriff released the three of them to their parents earlier this evening and next thing you know there's crosses burning all over town."

"Holy fright, what's next?" Dad said, "I heard those hooded hoodlums were getting stronger around here, but I thought it was just talk. I tell you, that old colored fella down the road better watch out. If they'll burn crosses in front of white kids houses, imagine what they'll do to a colored man for turning them in."

I caught Bud's look. He was just standing there listening, looking real grim. "Isaac Washington? Do you think they'd hurt him, Dad?" Bud asked.

"Those boys are a bunch of fanatics, no telling what they'll do next," Dad told him.

I walked over and wrapped my arms around Mom. All this talk was beginning to scare me. Mom looked down at me and told Dad and the boys why didn't they go out on the porch and finish talking. They did.

Kate and Lynn immediately headed upstairs. I knew what they were up to. If you opened up Kate's bedroom window sometimes you could hear what people were saying out on the porch.

"Momma, who are the hooded hoodlums and why would they burn crosses and hurt people?" I asked. It seemed to me they'd surely be some mean ones. They'd have to be in real trouble for those kinds of goings on. I hated to think what would happen to a person that burned a cross. I knew what Patty would say about this. "They'll burn in hell for sure!" she'd say.

Mom said not to be afraid that it was a terrible thing, but it didn't have anything to do with us. "We weren't around when all that went on," she said.

I got a real sinking feeling in my insides like somebody was in there twisting my stomach upside down and sideways. It was my bedtime, but Mom said I could sit with her a while on the couch. We sat down and I laid my head against her not really watching the television. As the black and white shadows from the screen bounced around the room Mom gently patted my hand on her lap and I felt warm and safe as I nestled to her side.

CHAPTER TEN

Rrroar! Rroar! I opened my eyes.

Rrroar! It was the lion alarm. I was real surprised to be in my bed. Dad must have brought me up. Lynn was curled up in a ball next to me. Her eyes were partly open, but I knew she was asleep. She slept with her eyes half open sometimes. It was the darndest thing. Just like a dead person on the television. One time Grandma Cummins stayed with us and slept with Lynn. One morning the whole house woke up to Grandma's screams, shortly followed by Lynn's. Grandma had awakened, taken one look at Lynn, and when she couldn't wake her, started screaming because she thought Lynn was dead. When we all got to Lynn's room, Grandma said, "She nearly gave me a heart attack, her eyes were wide open."

"You?" Lynn croaked, "I wake up to two beady little eyes about two inches from my nose and you say I nearly gave you a heart attack?"

"Your grandmother doesn't have beady eyes, Lynn," Mom corrected her, trying not to laugh.

I swear it was so funny. I had to leave the room. I couldn't remember how many times I had taken my friends in to watch Lynn sleep with her eyes like that. When I showed Patty she said we should take a picture of it.

The lion roared again, and Mom hollered up the stairs for us to get up. Lynn turned over her eyes open and awake now. Bud was downstairs already. I could hear him and Dad talking. When Lynn was good and awake, I asked her what she and Kate heard from the porch the night before. She looked at me like she didn't know what I was talking about.

"Come on Lynn, I know you guys came up to Kate's room to listen."

Lynn must have been tired cause she gave in too easy, "Not much other than Dad said for Bud to keep an eye on us girls and not let us go down to feed Lady and Satin anymore." Lady and Satin were Senator Collier's horses he let run in the pasture across from his home. We didn't know if that was their real names but that's the ones we gave them. Satin was black as night and her coat was shiny like Mrs. Thompson's mink coat.

Lady was a pretty roan that Kate said walked like royalty with her head held high in the air.

"How come we can't go there anymore?" I asked.

"With all this stuff happening around here Dad's worried something might come of those threats made on the senator," Lynn said. "He doesn't want us down there just in case. That's about all we heard, because Dad left then and walked down the road towards the boathouse. Kate and I think he went to check on the colored man."

"Well, what happened when Dad came back? Was Isaac okay?" I asked.

"I don't know. We went to bed before he came back," Lynn said.

"How could you go to bed without knowing if Dad came back or if Isaac was okay? If you two don't beat all," I told her, throwing my pillow at her.

"Oh Cally, don't be so dramatic. If something would have happened don't you think we would have heard something. Anyways, I think I heard Dad come back in. Everything was quiet. No crazy people running around burning crosses or anything around here last night," she said.

"Well, I want to go see Lady and Satin one more time to tell them goodbye," I said.

"You better wait awhile and see if things calm down first. Maybe Dad will forget about it," Lynn said.

CHAPTER ELEVEN

The days passed pretty uneventful the next few weeks. No more cross burnings, and no more incidents, at least as far as I knew. The kids that dug up the colored boy never did go to jail or nothing. Daddy said they probably just got a slap on the wrist because of who they were and all. Bud said that Tony was suspended a week for having the skull at school and they all three had to go to some Juvenile Hall counselor for a while. The only other mention of the whole incident was in the back of the newspaper. It said the colored community, and some ministers in town were outraged that more wasn't done to punish the kids and to bring the cross burners to justice. Dad and Mom were afraid there would be more trouble, but things stayed pretty quiet. For myself, I had decided it was high time I went down and introduced myself to Mr. Washington. He'd done me a good turn returning my candy and all, so I thought I'd thank him. Besides, I hadn't gone fishing in a while. I snuck my cane pole and a couple rubber worms from the bait box in the shed and headed to the boathouse.

Isaac was scooping minnows from the river into a bait bucket when I ambled up to the dock. "Excuse me," I said clearing my throat. He sort of cocked his head sideways so as to see whom it was. He placed the bucket on the dock and hands on his sides straightened up ever so slowly.

"Well now, who have we here?" he said, walking a little closer.

I backed up. I wasn't too sure this was a good idea now that we were face to face and all.

"Cally Cummins," I said holding my fishing pole in front of me as if it would protect me from some unknown attacker.

"Cummins? Cummins," he repeated tapping his finger on his stubbly chin. "Bud's sister!

"Yes sir," I said, relieved to hear Bud's name.

"Didn't recognize you in the light of day," he smiled slyly. "That's a mighty fine cane pole you got there Cally Cummins," he said. "Can't catch them big bass with nothing better. A cane pole and a piece of balled up bread with Black Strap molasses to hold it together draws them fish like bees to honey." I watched him as he talked on about fishing and the river. He seemed full of excitement at the prospect of it all. He waved his arms pretending to cast his line. Then he strained, pulling back and forth battling the one that nearly got away, yanking the invisible catch to the dock. He motioned for me to follow and led me to a deep black pool in the midst of knarled up cypress knees. "There's a big one in there got your name on it, Cally. This here is the best spot along here," he said. Holding up one long bony finger he told me, "I'll be back in a minute."

By and by he was beside me again. This time he had a bag of little dough balls covered all over with an amber substance.

"Try one of these on your line," he said.

Sticking it on my hook I held up sticky fingers.

"It's just molasses, wash it off in the water," he said. Instead, I licked the powerful sweet stuff clean off. Isaac hooted. We fished until suppertime. I caught two brim, but gave them to Isaac. He said he'd clean them up and if I came back he'd fry them up for him and me. Well, I came back again and again. After school I'd finish up my studies and head to the boathouse. So as not to have to sneak it out, I left my pole there. We fished and Isaac fried up our catches in corn meal and lard. Mom started to wonder if I was getting poorly when I couldn't eat my usual fill at the supper table. We had a glorious time, Isaac and me. We'd fish and feed the beautiful Wood Ducks that swam in the canal. Sometimes Isaac's old fishing buddy and lifelong friend, Tyson would come over. Tyson was a very round, bulky man with a contagious laugh. He'd tell us the best jokes, and bring me fireballs from the grocery. The three of us had a grand time. The two colored men talked of their families and how they used to live in the shanties and work the groves and fish the St. Johns together. I got around to asking Isaac about his dearly departed grandmother, and if she was in the colored cemetery like Jack Jackson said. Isaac kind of got a far away look and I thought I caught a tear in his brown eyes. He looked down at the canal then shook his head saying, "Yes, Miss Cally, she is. God rest her pure tired old soul." That's all he said about it.

The two colored men got a rip-roaring laugh when I asked them about the colored spirits chasing white folks around on Halloween. They never did answer me. Isaac just rubbed the top of my head and said, "You just beat all, Cally Cummins," and laughed some more.

In those lazy river days I discovered Isaac was not only an excellent fisherman, but was pretty handy with a knife; a carving one that is. One day when I got there ready to settle in on my favorite spot, I spied a little carved duck sitting on the pier post. It was whittled right out of a pine-cone. It had a note attached with my name on it, tied with wire around its neck. I kept it locked up in my closet in the yellow Havana Cigar Box Dad gave me after he'd finished the last.

Autumn days quickly passed and I nearly had put the events of October behind, until the Saturday before Thanksgiving.

It was the first crisp day we had had. The air was cool, but not nippy. Bud and Larry put on their windbreakers and headed outside. When I asked them where they were going this time they didn't tell me a story, but said they were going down to see Isaac. They hadn't been down there in a good while, lucky for me. I asked Bud if I could go along. Lynn and Kate were in town with friends and I was at a loss for something to do. I asked Bud to please let me come. He said he didn't know why I was asking him for, being as I was down there all the time anyways.

"Doggone it Bud, how'd you know? You been spying on me?" I asked.

"What's good for one's good for the other, ain't it?" Bud smirked.

"So then, now you know. Can I come along or not?" I asked.

Bud said he supposed so as long as I didn't get in to anything.

We walked along the paved road and I told Bud about me and Isaac and how he showed me the secret fishing hole and about the duck. I was glad somebody knew and I could talk about my new friend. I wasn't too sure what Mom and Dad would say about me hanging around down there. So, I'd kept my secret 'til then. As I walked along I got to thinking how Isaac was the only colored folk I'd ever talked to. That is except for the old man that always sat outside Pierson's grocery in town.

Sometimes on Saturdays I'd ride with Dad to Piersons to pick up some Mail Pouch tobacco for him to chew while he worked on the house. The old man would be sitting outside and when we'd come out, Dad would say, "Afternoon," or "Nice day," and the old man would nod and say, "Afternoon" back, or, "mighty fine day, mighty fine." He always had a bulge in his cheek full of brown tobacco juice that sometimes would trickle down his chin from the corner of his mouth. But those spoken words really didn't count because it was Dad talking, not me. Isaac was my friend. If all colored folks were like the old man at the grocery, and Isaac and Tyson, then they surely must be good people.

We had to pass the Collier place on the way to the boathouse. I thought I might get a chance to see Lady and Satin if they were out. When we got to the pasture gate Satin wasn't there, but Lady was and there was a girl riding her. The girl had long dark hair pulled back in a ribbon, and had the queerest outfit on. Her pants had big puffy legs that ended at the top of big tall black boots that ran clean up to her knees. On her head she wore one of those sporty little caps like Grandpa Looney (pronounced low-knee) wore when he drove his MG. She held her head high just like Lady's.

"Well, I wonder who the heck that is riding Lady, Bud? I never saw anyone riding the horses before," I said leaning on the gate. Watching Lady galloping across the field I said, "Isn't she beautiful? She looks just like one of those you see in the pictures from England. You know? The ones that chase after those little foxes."

"Yeah, she's beautiful all right," Bud said, staring. He had a real sick grin on his face like he'd just eaten too many Musketeer bars.

"Oh brother, I meant Lady, not the girl," I said, shoving him against the gate.

The girl rode towards us now and Bud and Larry stood there pulling their shoulders back and sucking in their guts, puffing their chests out like a couple banty roosters.

"Hello," the girl said.

"Hello yourself," Larry said, Bud just standing there grinning that dumb grin.

"I'm Gloria Collier, who might you all be?" she asked very grown-up like.

Larry spoke up. "I'm Larry Voight, and this here is Bud Cummins. Bud lives down the road in the Jackson house."

How do you like that I thought? "Ah HMMM!" I cleared my throat. Larry and Bud looked at me like I had just appeared out of nowhere.

"Oh, and this is my little sister, Cally," Bud just sort of tossed in there like I was an old shoe or something.

"Where's Satin?" I asked. The girl looked at me all confused like. Then I remembered she probably didn't call the horse Satin.

"The black horse that's always out here with Lady," I said. Now she really looked confused. Now I was too. I tried to explain, "We call the black horse Satin and the one you're riding, Lady."

"Oh, that's Caesar. I'm not allowed to ride him. He was my mother's horse. She was the only one who could keep him under control," she said.

"I didn't know Senator Collier had any kids," Bud said. Gloria explained, "Ever since my Mother died two years ago I've been going to a boarding school in New England. I'm home for Thanksgiving." Then she said to me, "You must really like my horses, Cally to have taken the time to pick out names for them and come visit."

I was impressed she remembered my name.

"Maybe you and your brother would like to go riding one day while I'm home."

"That would be great," Bud said. Larry looked like a lost puppy. "You too, Larry, if you like," she told him. He perked right up.

"Hey, why don't you come over later and meet my sisters, Lynn and Kate. Kate is in ninth grade," I said.

"Cally, don't be so pushy," Bud warned.

"I think that would be nice, Cally. I'm in the tenth grade so I think Kate, Bud and I might have a lot in common," Gloria said, looking at Bud, not me.

Bud's face was getting all red. "We've got to be going now," he said.

"Yeah, we'll call you later and you can come over. Maybe you can come for supper," I said.

"Cally, we need to go," Bud said.

"I'll be waiting," Gloria said.

"Cally, one of these days I'm going to choke the life right out of you," Bud threatened when we got out of Gloria's ear shot. "You're so damned forward.

"What's the matter with you Bud? I've never seen you act so weird around a girl. You're not that shy around the girls you know from your school," I told him.

"She's not like the girls at school," Bud said. "No kidding? I think it's what Kate calls having class. I can't quite picture Gloria in leopard skin," I teased.

"I don't know what you're complaining about Buddy boy. I wish I had a little sister to invite gorgeous girls to my house," Larry said. Bud socked Larry in the arm.

As we approached the boathouse there was an old black pick-up parked outside. Two shotguns sat perched in the gun racks in its back window. Just when we got to the door loud angry voices could be heard inside. Bud stopped, "What's going on in there?" He said in a hushed voice.

I motioned the boys to follow me around to the side of the building where Patty and I had spied on them before.

The voices were much clearer now. They were out near the docks. Larry boosted me up on Bud's shoulders so I could look inside.

"You don't hear too well do ya' nigger," a big sloppy fat man in a hunting jacket said. He was poking a finger in Isaac's chest, "I thought we made it real clear that you were to move on after you turned in old Zeke here's niece and those boys."

"I didn't do nothing wrong. You fellas ain't got no right coming in here like this," Isaac said his voice shaking.

"You hear that Zeke? We ain't got no right," the fat one said again. The two of them started doubling over laughing.

"What's happening Cally?" Bud whispered.

"Shhh, I can't hear. The two men are yelling at Isaac and…"

"We can hear that, what are they doing?" Bud said irritated.

They're bending over laughing now, but the big fat one was poking Isaac in the chest earlier. Wait a minute Bud, the fat one just grabbed Isaac by the shirt.

"This here badge gives me the right to do whatever I want with you, Boy," he said, holding Isaac with one hand and pointing at his badge with the other.

"Isaac looks real scared, Bud. That one man just locked Isaac's neck in the crook of his arm." I said.

"We gotta do something Larry. We can't just sit here," Bud said.

"Don't you go doing nothing yet, Bud Cummins. You want to get your fool head blown off or something?" I said getting scared.

"Wait. Just a second," I said holding up a hand. "They let Isaac go. Hey, that fat one just pushed him down." I was getting worried now. "What can we do Buddy?" I said.

The skinny one the fat one had called Zeke said, "If you don't get your nigger ass out of here we'll fix you good you hear? We'll go teaching you to turn in my flesh and blood."

"If you was so upset about it, why'd you go burning crosses in her yard and those boys?" asked Isaac.

"Well, now how do you know it was our boys? Maybe it was some of you nigger boys trying to make it look like our brothers of the Klan did it. Yeah! That's what it was. Don't you believe so Eugene?" The one named Zeke said.

"Those dirty S.O.B.'s," Larry said.

"You fellas know it wasn't no colored man did that," Isaac told them.

"Well, if it was the Klan," the Zeke fella' said, "and I ain't saying it was, they done it 'cause the only good nigger is a dead nigger. Once in the ground that's where they should stay. As far as them crosses go, that Jew boy and that wop got what they deserved. The boys might have got carried away, didn't know it was a brother's blood; a good white protestant girl. That's why I say maybe it was the coloreds done it, so the law would blame it on the Klan."

"You'll pay for that one, you and the rest," the fat one said.

"You're gonna find yourself in that there cemetery boy if you give us any more trouble and don't leave. We'll fix you one way or the other. We'll fix you good," Skinny Zeke said poking Isaac again.

"Bud they're leaving, put me down," I said, nearly falling off his shoulders in my hurry.

Putting me safely to the ground, Bud went running back towards the front of the building, "Come on, let's get a better look at them," he said.

When we got close to the front corner we lay on our bellies hiding behind an oleander bush. When the men came out their backs were to us and there were three instead of two. As the third one turned a shiver ran through me, "Bud," I said, "It's Roy Peterson, Hal's daddy."

"Let's get around back before they pull out and see us," Bud said.

We waited until the truck was well down the road before checking Isaac. Poor old Isaac was so scared shiny streams of sweat shimmered down his dark skin. His hands were trembling as he sat on the side of the dock looking down into the dark water. He turned with a start when he heard our footsteps on the wooden planks.

"What are you kids doing here?" Isaac rasped, obviously shaken.

"Are you okay Isaac. You don't look so good," Larry said.

"We saw the men Isaac and we heard every rotten thing they said to you. What are you going to do about it? Maybe you should call the sheriff," Bud said.

"Can't call the law, boy; that was the law," Isaac said as he shook his head. Isaac tried to stand, but his legs didn't want to hold him and he sat back down.

"He's just some big-mouthed red-neck deputy, not the sheriff," Bud told Isaac holding his arm out for Isaac to pull up on.

"I don't know boy, I think it's time to move on, go and stay with what family I got in Ocala," Isaac said standing now, but still not real steady.

"They're just gonna' find some other poor colored folks to scare. Seems like there's something can be done," Bud said frustration growing in his voice.

"Nothing will be done 'til something real bad happens, and people get fed up with those devils and their terrorizing. Then the law will step in, when it's too late. That's just the way it is. You're young. You'll learn," Isaac said. Isaac held a long bony finger up in front of Bud. I never really noticed how weathered Isaac's hands were from years of work and wear. I thought it odd for such a small man to have such large hands and long fingers. They were a hard working man's hands, like my dad's. As he pointed he said, "You let old Isaac worry about all this stuff. You're good kids. You best not be coming down here no more. I talked to your Daddy the other night when all that trouble came about in town. He's a good man. He and your Momma would be mighty upset with me if I allowed you down here and something happened to you. It's just plain trouble here and no good can come of it. Now don't you kids be saying nothing to nobody. I'll take care of it."

"But, Isaac," Bud started, but Isaac interrupted.

"No buts boy, this ain't no kid's play, you hear? This is best for now."

"Yes sir," Bud said then took off.

"Isaac?" I said.

Isaac stopped me with a raised hand and said, "No arguments Cally. If anything happened to you or your brother and Larry, I couldn't live with myself. Now get on home and mind what I say."

I hugged his overalls and he lightly patted the top of my head. Larry's hand gently pulled me, "Come on Cal, it's time to go."

Bud stayed ahead of Larry and me the whole way back to the Jackson place. One time I started to try and catch up with him, but Larry grabbed my shoulder and we walked on home without speaking so much as a word. Larry kept his hand strong on my shoulder the whole way back.

Bud ran straight in the house when he got there. Larry stayed in the living room with me and turned on the television set. He didn't even try to look for Bud. He was staring at the set, but I didn't think he was really watching it. On the screen some fat woman was showing how to cook fried chicken. Just about the time the woman was serving up a delicious looking platter Larry got up and said to tell Bud he'd talk to him later and left. That's all he said the whole time. I was kind of glad. I'd heard enough talk. I turned the channel to Tarzan.

Kate and Lynn came home with Dad from town. When Mom called us to supper, Bud said he wasn't hungry. Bud and I didn't call Gloria, but I told everyone about her at supper, and Mom called the senator that evening and invited Gloria to Sunday dinner after church the next day.

CHAPTER TWELVE

Bud didn't have to go to church with us, and Momma let him sleep in. During the service I couldn't get old Isaac off my mind or those awful men. I wouldn't have blamed Isaac if he high tailed it. I'd miss him something terrible, but I rather have him safe in Ocala than…I didn't want to think about it. Those awful men could put the fear in any man, or child for that matter.

When church was over I took an extra red and white peppermint from the bowl in the church vestibule for Bud. When he was unwrapping it later I asked him why those men had called Isaac a nigger, and what exactly one was.

"Cally, don't you ever let me hear you say that word again," Bud yelled at me.

"Well, that's what they called him, and that's the same thing Hal Peterson said the new girl from New York loved. Hal called her a damn Yankee and said she should go back up North with the rest of the nigger lovers. Hal's got names like those for just about everybody different than himself. What is it Bud?" I asked.

"It's something that will get your mouth washed out with soap again if you let Momma and Daddy hear you say it," Bud said. He told me, "No, Isaac isn't one of those. It's just a word ignorant people call coloreds. Men like we saw yesterday and their ill taught kids."

I decided I better change the subject and asked Bud if he would come downstairs when Gloria came over for Sunday dinner. "She should be here any minute," I told him.

His face lit up; "I'm getting pretty hungry, so I guess I could come down for awhile," he said.

I knew darn well he wouldn't miss that for anything. Pretty soon the biggest black car I'd ever seen pulled up in the driveway. Lynn, Kate and I stared out the curtains as the driver got out, dressed in black from head to toe, his hat pulled down over his eyes. He opened the back door of the car and out stepped Gloria.

"For crying out loud don't stare at her like that," Bud said coming down the steps. We moved away, and Bud took our place at the window.

"They must be the richest people in River County," I told Mom.

"Her Daddy's a politician. I hear they have all the money," Dad said.

"Oh Will!" Mom said, giving Dad her "be good or else" look.

Bud answered the door. There was that sick grin again, but at least he was smiling now.

Gloria looked even prettier than she did riding her horse. Standing, she was as tall as Kate was and thin like her too. Her black hair fell loose around her shoulders and she wore a wide red hair band in it. All her clothes matched, from her pleated skirt and red jacket to her shoes. Definitely not Sears Roebuck I thought. Gloria's green eyes sparkled as she smiled at Bud. I whispered to Kate, "Don't you think she looks just like Veronica in the Archie comics?"

Kate whispered back, "You always think people look like movie stars or cartoon characters. Don't you go telling her that, like the time you told Aunt Jen that Carla looked like Pebbles on that new show "The Flintstones." You know how that went over."

"I meant she was a cute baby, and I happen to think Betty and Veronica are pretty," I told her.

"Like I've said before, you're weird, Cally," Kate said walking over to Bud who introduced Gloria to her and the family.

Mom made my favorite for dinner. Roast beef, with brown pan gravy, carrots and potatoes. Everyone was on their best behavior. Dad didn't mention politics once and Bud didn't reach across or belch or anything. Not that we were allowed to do that, but sometimes a kid forgot. Like Cousin George did the time we were visiting them up in Jacksonville. He reached across in front of Uncle Al for a second helping of mashed potatoes, and Uncle Al stuck a fork in the top of his hand. Not all the way through or nothing, just pricked the top a little. George's middle name was Marrot, which we'd never heard him called before. When Uncle Al stuck him he said, "George Marrot McMann!" Bud thought he said Parrot and busted out laughing. Pretty soon all us kids were out on the porch without dessert. No, this time we were all on our best behavior for Gloria, and Mom's cherry pie.

After dinner Dad and Mom said they would take care of the dishes so us kids could entertain our guest. For a rich girl Gloria was real sweet and fit right in, though she talked a little fancier. Kate said it was boarding school talk. Mom and Dad seemed to like her real well. I knew they would. She was real polite to them and told Mom what a terrific cook she was.

Sunday afternoons out in the country run slow and easy like the river. There's not much to do except go fishing or hiking. Everything is closed up in town except the Freeze-ette and a couple gas stations. This afternoon was no exception. We kids were just kind of lolly-gaggin out on the porch. Kate brought down the Chinese checkers. After one game, Mom and Dad came out in their work clothes and said they were going to the new house for awhile.

"You kids behave and stay out of mischief. It will probably be around supper time when we get back," Mom said. She gave me a kiss on top of my head and added, "You listen to your brother Cally, and mind what he tells you."

"Yes ma'am," I said trying to imitate Gloria's manners.

When they had gone Lynn said, "Let's go for a walk or something. It's boring just sitting around on the porch playing checkers."

"Hey Buddy, why don't you take us to that old hotel down by the river you said Jack Jackson told you about," Kate suggested.

"That place is about two miles from here Kate. If I know ya'll we'll walk all that way and you'll chicken out because it's supposed to be haunted," he said.

"I'll go Bud," I said.

"Haunted? I don't know Bud," Lynn said. Then her worried look changed to a smile suddenly and she said, "We can't, Gloria's not dressed for it."

"My house is just down the road. Dad insisted our chauffeur, Victor drive me here, but honestly it's only a few houses away. I can run home and change and be back before you know it," she said.

"I've got a better idea," Kate said, "We're about the same size. You can wear something of mine. The two girls ran up to change. Bud went in and filled up a jug with icewater for us to take along. When everyone was ready we followed Bud across the road into the sandy field. The afternoon sun felt warm compared to the chilly November morning we'd woke to. I was glad I wore long pants, because the grass and weeds in the field were pretty high. I was afraid of tics. They used to get on our old dog Major. Bud would have to pull them out of Major's ears with a pair of Dad's pliers. It was all pretty disgusting. The doggone sandspurs and beggarlytes stuck to my pant legs and socks bad enough without having to worry about tics too. Finally out of the tall weeds and into the sandy citrus grove we stopped and pulled the spurs off so they wouldn't scratch our legs up."

Looking around, the oranges here seemed much bigger. I could just taste the acidy sweetness.

"Look over there," Bud said, pointing to an old cabin in the thick brush, sheltered under the dark shadows of the tall pines at the edge of the grove. "Doesn't appear to be lived in," Bud said.

The windows we could see were busted out and the roof sagged towards its middle. Bud was just about there with Gloria sticking close behind him. The front door was off its hinges and just leaning against the walls. Bud was about to go in when Kate told him he better not because the whole place might cave in on him.

"It's been here a long time by the looks of it. I don't think today is the day it's gonna cave in," Bud said.

Gloria kind of tip-toed in behind Bud, ducking her head like something was about to fall on it. Kate sort of huffed, but went in just the same. Lynn and I were about to enter when Kate let out a scream that sent chills up my back. She came flying out almost knocking Lynn and I over.

"Don't go in there. There's the ugliest most hideous looking thing in there," she said. You could hear Bud laughing. Gloria came out almost as fast as Kate did.

"What is that thing?" she squealed, looking at where she had been, not where she was going, running into the back of Kate. Both of them bolted away from the cabin and turned, watching the door like they were expecting something horrible to come after them.

Bud's laughter was louder now. He came to the door holding by the tail the ugliest spiny looking green lizard I'd ever seen. It wasn't small like the chameleons we saw all the time. This thing was at least a foot long. It had a bumpy back and it flung itself back and forth trying to get loose.

"Bud Cummins, put that thing down and let's go," Kate yelled.

"It's just an old lizard, Kate. Hey, maybe we can keep him for a pet," he teased. At least I hoped he was.

"Mom would skin you alive if you brought that thing in the house," Kate said. "Now just drop it Buddy!"

He put it back down inside the doorway, and turned back real fast towards Kate and Gloria, running at them and holding a stick in his hand instead of the miniature Godzilla. They hooped and hollered something awful and ran back the way we had come from. Me, Bud and Lynn laughed so hard I thought I'd better sit down. They were a sight.

Bud said we'd better catch up to them before they ran all the way home. When we caught up, Kate got in a mood, but Gloria wanted to continue our walk. So Kate came along, but she wouldn't talk to any of us until we reached the railroad tracks.

"Which way do we go from here?" Kate kind of snotty asked Bud.

"Back towards the left there," Bud said.

"I thought the swamp was down there," Kate told him.

"Yeah, Mr. Jackson said we had to cross over it on the tracks, then it's just a ways further to the dirt road that runs to the river and the old hotel," Bud said.

We walked on, Kate mumbling something about getting snake bit.

"Hey, did I tell you I'm buying Jack Jackson's car Tuesday night after work," Bud said as we walked along the track. Now Kate perked up. Free rides into town obviously took away her mood.

"I've saved more than enough for the payment and now the 'galloping ghost' will be mine," he said.

"What's the 'galloping ghost'?" asked Gloria. "Jack Jackson's old gray Plymouth. That's what Mom calls it," Bud told her.

"That's great, Bud. Your own car and all, I mean," Gloria said.

"I can't wait to drive her by myself. Maybe I'll come by and give you a ride," he told Gloria.

"AH HMMM!" I said. Bud looked at me and said, "After I give Cally a ride."

"And Me and Lynn," Kate chimed in.

Bud was red-faced again. "Would you like three sisters, I'll sell them cheap," Bud said to Gloria.

"What do you suppose we'll find in that old hotel anyway?" Lynn asked. You could tell she still wasn't too keen on this whole adventure.

"Probably more of those disgusting lizards," Kate said. We continued walking and we came to a big wide curve in the tracks. It seemed like we had been walking for hours. We stopped for a drink from the jug Bud brought along. You could see way on the other side of the curve that the tracks straightened out and the trestles climbed up over the swamp.

"What if we fall off," Kate said, looking towards the trestles.

"I knew it, I knew we'd get all this way and you'd start chickening out. I at least thought you'd wait 'til we got to the hotel," Bud said.

"I've gone this far," he said, "I'm going across. Stay here if you want. Who's coming?" Bud turned and asked.

"Come on Kate. We've come this far," Gloria coaxed.

"I don't think we should be taking Cally over that," Kate said.

"I'll be fine, come on Kate," I said. "I don't have a good feeling about this," she said grabbing my hand and walking after Bud.

All right! I thought. We were a little over halfway across when we heard it, a whistle, just off in the distance. Kate's grip clamped down stronger.

"Damn, a train!" Bud hollered. "Everybody move it." Kate pulled on my arm tighter now.

"Kate slow down. It's a long way down and I'm getting dizzy looking through these ties," I told her as she pulled me along.

Lynn was between Gloria and Bud and she tripped, falling forward. Bud grabbed her up. The whistles were coming faster and louder now. I could feel a rumble in the wooden planks between the rails.

"Just a little further Cally," Kate now had a death grip on my hand and it ached. Bud, Lynn and Gloria were across. The whistle screamed closer.

"Come on Kate. Hurry up!" Bud pleaded madly waving his arms at us.

I turned to look behind us and the black and silver locomotive had just made it to the curve.

Kate told me to quit looking back and gave me one final jerk and we were on the other side.

"Now where Bud?" Kate cried breathlessly, looking wildly down the steep grade of ground leading up from the swamp to the tracks. Tears streamed down her cheeks.

"Everybody, down on your hands and knees and crawl off the track backward onto the slope," Bud ordered. Everyone scrambled off. As we lay on our bellies in the slope's tall grass Kate pulled me close to her and the train rumbled closer.

The ground shook so hard I thought I just might slide into the swamp below. The sound was deafening. I looked at Kate through my watery eyes and she was sobbing. The train was so close I could feel the breeze as the huge blurry metal monster rocked and creaked as it screamed above us. The red caboose was safely off in the distance before anyone moved or said a word. A few mild whimpers could be heard from Kate's direction.

"Everybody all right?" Bud's voice shouted from the other side of the tracks.

"We're fine," Kate sniffed and cleared her throat, "Let's go Cally. Bud, let's go home," Kate said crawling back up to the tracks above us. She turned and stooped down giving me her hand to pull up on. Bud was looking down the track the direction the train had gone.

"Kate, there's the road. Look over there by that tallest pine; the one with the eagle's nest in the top," Bud said pointing.

Sure enough it was the dirt road. "Come on Kate, there won't be anymore trains this afternoon. Remember there's always one about supper time," Bud assured her.

I took her hand and we walked slowly towards the others.

Off the tracks now the dirt road in front of us was like a long dusty tunnel. Moss draped down from the tree limbs that curved overhead. Every once in a while a flicker of sunlight shone through the mossy cover. I thought I heard a rattler off in the distance and an old gator croaked down by the river. He sounded like a giant bullfrog.

The road turned into a bed of slippery pine needles and cones spread across the sand. Hidden in amongst the pines, its brownish gray peeling paint blending in with the trees was the old ramshackle hotel. It was three stories high and made at least two of the Jackson house. There was an old tin roofed garage separate from the hotel.

We all ran up to the rickety porch that ran around two sides of the place. Part of an old dock still ran down to the river's edge from the porch.

Bud stood, hands on his hips, taking in the place, "Must have been a pretty neat hotel in its heyday. People must have pulled up there along the dock when they were traveling the river. Jack Jackson said there was illegal gambling here back in those days. Nobody bothered them way out here. The law just looked the other way I suppose."

I was peeking in the window looking up at a big skylight that looked out through the roof. There was an opening all the way up from the main floor. The other two floors had balconies looking over the first floor.

"I wonder if that's where they hung those colored boys," I said and everyone came over to look.

"Nice Cally, that's a pleasant thought," Kate said irritated.

"Well, Jack Jackson said it happened and so did the newspaper. I was just wondering if they hung them up there," I said pointing to the skylight.

Bud tried to open the front door, but it was locked. The window I was looking through wasn't locked and slid up pretty easy, so we all climbed in.

"Bud, I don't know if we should be doing this. There was a sign posted outside that said 'No Trespassing,'" Kate said after we already had crawled in.

"It's probably just there to keep people from getting hurt," Bud said.

"I don't think anyone's been here for a while. There's not one piece of furniture or anything," Gloria said.

"That's what you think. Look in here," Kate said standing at the door she had just opened.

On the other side of the door was a room with nothing but wooden folding chairs stacked up against each other and a wooden stand that looked like a church pulpit. It even had a wooden cross on it.

"Jack Jackson mentioned this was some kind of hunt club now, not a church. I wonder what a hunt club would be doing with a pulpit," Bud said.

Looking further we found other odd things in the room. A small box of medals with crosses on their fronts, and some other strange markings etched into the crosses' centers, sat on a shelf inside the back of the pulpit.

"Must be some church group using this place," I said.

"Way out here? That's pretty strange, like they're ashamed of what they do or something," Lynn said.

Inside a closet was an American flag, a Confederate flag and another one we couldn't figure out, but it had a cross on it too. A sword rested in one corner of the closet and there was a box full of long burlap strips.

Bud said, "I think we better get on out of here. This place isn't as deserted as we thought. I just want to look in that old garage before we go."

Crawling back through the window, the sun had gone down noticeably and it was a little cooler since we had first got there.

"We better hurry up Bud. We have a long walk back before dark," Kate said.

Bud ran over to the old garage and looked inside a clouded window. He came back quickly. His voice was a little edgy as he told us he was ready to go. We hurried down the tunneled road and were back to the tracks in no time.

After we made it over the trestles and were safely on flat ground again Kate asked Bud what had been in the garage.

"I'm not sure Kate. Looked like a bunch of wooden poles, gasoline cans, a case of motor oil and some more of them burlap strips. I just got a real uneasy feeling when I was over there. Something is real peculiar about this place. There's something else I found in that little room. He pulled out a piece of folded up paper from his pocket.

"Look at this," he showed us the paper. At the top of the page was a list of strange names and beside them were names of men.

Cyclops: Marshall Hall

Klaliff: Ben Smitt

Kligrapp: Roy Peterson

I stopped reading there. There went those chills again. Bud said, "Look at this list of dates here. This one here," he pointed to the paper and read, "November 23, that's Tuesday night." He folded the paper up and put it back in his pocket.

It was just beginning to get dark when we reached the citrus grove again. The moon was full and shimmered against the white sand like a giant flashlight. It's real odd how the same noises you heard during the light of day take on a whole different feeling after dark. At night, bugs flittin' and rabbits scampering become rattlers and bobcats. A sand spur sticks in your leg and you swear you've been snake bit.

It was getting cold and I was hungry. Enormous, plump oranges dangled from the low citrus branches. I felt like a caged jackrabbit in a carrot patch looking at them. They surely were just right for the pickin'. Too much longer and they'd fall off and not be good to anyone. I didn't recall seeing any keep out signs over here.

"Mom and Dad are home," Lynn said. Across the road warm light glowed through ruffled curtains. Hot roast beef sandwiches and potato patties sounded real good right now.

Bud and Gloria were lagging behind the rest of us. Their voices were soft and low, and their quiet laughter sounded foreign all mixed in with the night's sounds.

We were just about to the paved road when the front door opened and Mom stepped out on the now lighted porch. Her eyes searched the darkness.

"Over here Mom, across the road," Kate called out. Kate broke into a run, "Last one there's a rotten egg," she hollered.

Laughing and out of breath we raced to the porch and Mom. Bud and Gloria were the rotten eggs. Somehow, I didn't think they cared.

"Buddy and Gloria seem to be getting pretty fond of one another," Mom said craning her head to see the two walking across the road and up the walk.

"Maybe he'll forget about Sheanna of the Jungle," I said. Mom, never taking her eyes off of them, smiled slightly and raised her eyebrows as if to agree.

"Gloria, your father called and wanted to know when you'd be home. I told him you might as well stay for supper and Bud can take you home afterwards, if that's okay with you," Mom said as the two rotten eggs got to the porch.

Gloria looked at Bud all gushy like and said that it would be fine. As we all headed inside a train whistle could be heard off in the distance.

Soon supper was ready and Mom said for us to come on in and wash up. Nobody argued with that. I could almost taste it already, my stomach growling.

It seemed an unusually long supper prayer tonight. I kept eyein' the potato patties 'til Dad caught me lookin', and gave me his evil eye.

"Amen," Mom said.

Dad picked up the patties and was about to pass them my way, then hesitated, looking at me slyly. "I think we'll start over here," he said passing them down to Kate.

I thought I'd pass out or something when they finally got to me. As Lynn was handing me the platter Dad asked, "So what did you all do this afternoon?" I was trying to stab a pattie, when Bud kicked me under the table. That was my signal to keep quiet, but he needn't worry about that I was too hungry to blab.

Bud summed up the afternoon for us. It was a pretty quiet one to hear him tell it; Chinese checkers, some television, and a walk to see what was across the field. No lizards, swamps, trains or haunted hotels in this version of our day.

Dad said all the necessary outside work was done on the house and the men were coming to start wiring it tomorrow. "It won't be long now," he said. "We can start putting up the inside walls, and plastering soon."

"I can't wait," Kate said, "Back to civilization." After supper Bud drove Gloria home in the family car. While we were doing dishes Lynn said she bet Bud would kiss Gloria goodnight. Mom told her it wasn't proper to kiss on the first date.

"Well, it's not exactly a date," Lynn said. "Well, I say if you like somebody and they like you, why not kiss em," I said. "Shoot, the boys are always chasing us girls on the playground and trying to kiss us. I could beat any one of them in a fair race, but if I like them, I run slower."

"Cally Cummins, I can see right now I'm going to have to keep a close eye on you when you get old enough to date," Mom said, hands on her hips.

"Honestly Mom, Cally's going to be a handful one of these days if you and Dad don't start getting after her more," Kate said. "She gets away with more than any of the rest of us."

Sometimes I just said stuff to get Mom and especially Kate all riled up. Lynn and I got a big kick out of it. It didn't take much to do it either, especially on topics such as the proper way to behave. Mom wasn't too bad. She just didn't want me to be a juvenile delinquent. But Kate, oh brother. Mom said it was just that phase grandma said Kate was going through, and that all teenage girls were skittish and worried about what everyone thought all the time. Kate was always afraid I'd do something to embarrass her.

Bud got back after Walt Disney. He was whistling when he came in the back door.

"He kissed her," Lynn said, and she and I started laughing.

"Now hush girls," Mom scolded as Bud came in the room.

"Well Buddy, did you meet the Senator?" Dad asked. Bud sat on the ottoman in front of Dad's chair.

"Yes sir, and he's a pretty nice guy. He invited me in when I took Gloria to the door. He's got the biggest collection of baseball cards I ever saw. He's got a Stan Musial," Bud said.

Dad raised his eyebrows in approval. Bud said, "Do you know they have a security guy lives there now? Gloria said he's been working there since her daddy started getting all them threats. Gloria's real worried about him, and doesn't want to go back up to school. She asked him could she transfer to DHS. Hope she does."

Dad smiled, "I'll bet you do son. Seems to me though it would be awful lonesome for her here with her daddy being gone up to the state capitol in Tallahassee so much."

"Buddy would keep her company," Lynn said giggling.

Bud flashed her a one-two punch look and said, "Her daddy's dead set against her staying here."

"Can't say I blame him for that Bud, she's all he's got and he's not a very popular man right now in some notorious circles. Some of those fanatics out there can be pretty treacherous with people they feel cross them and, these local yokels are nothing compared to what's going on around the rest of the country. Believe me she's better off up in New England or wherever it is she goes to school," Dad told Bud.

Bud sort of shrugged and said he was going upstairs to do his homework. Ed Sullivan came on and Dad leaned back in his chair. That goofy little mouse Topo Giogio was on with Mr. Sullivan so I decided I'd go up and read my new Nancy Drew book.

CHAPTER THIRTEEN

It was finally Tuesday, the last day of school before our Thanksgiving holiday. Miss Rowell took roll call, then told us to take out our mathematics books. It figures, I thought on the last day before a holiday she'd go and make us do times tables. Hal Peterson came in late his head hangin' hangdog low. He walked over and handed Miss Rowell a crumpled up note he had dug out of his shirt pocket. She looked at the note, then took her hand and raised his face to her. We couldn't see Hal's face, but Miss Rowell's usually sharp pointed features relaxed and her cold stern eyes softened. She told him to have a seat. Hal drooped his head again and turned, shuffling to his desk and shoved his reader underneath into the cubby hole. Miss Rowell didn't even say nothing mean to him for interrupting our math lesson. When recess came Hal lagged behind the rest of us as we filed out to the playground. I did manage to see in one little instant when he got out of his seat the big purply black shiner he had on his left eye. His eye looked like a tiny speck in the middle of all that puffy blue black skin. Hal stayed pretty much to himself over by the basketball court playing with his bag of marbles.

"You get a good look at Hal. I'll bet he smarted off to his daddy again and got beat. He's such a snot," Susan Baines said. "Nobody deserves that kind of beatin', not even Hal Peterson. His daddy ought to be horse-whipped for what he does to his boy," I said, surprising myself for sticking up for Hal.

"What's got into you Cally?" Patty asked.

"Nothing, I just don't think it's right, that's all." I went over to the swings, and swung up as high as I could until the chains rattled and the swing jumped. Then remembering the time Bud went over the bars, I quit pumping so hard. All the while I swung I watched Hal flicking his marbles across the sand by the court. I decided I would try and talk to him. I wasn't sure why, but it seemed like the thing to do. Besides, I was curious as to what happened to him. I jumped from the swing seat. It was the best bail out yet, I sailed at least six feet. Walking over to the basketball court I got a good look at just how big the bruise was. Hal put his head down when he saw me coming.

"Your eye hurt real bad?" I asked.

"Just go on and get on out of here, Cally. I don't need your sympathy," Hal snapped.

"Well, you don't have to bite my head off." I was just asking, I said, "How'd you do it?"

"None of your damn business," he snarled. I could feel the back of my neck getting hot.

"For two cents I'd black your other eye for ya," I said, walking away mad at myself for feeling sorry for the likes of him.

"Ouch!" I said, something hitting the back of my head. Turning I could see Hal grinning, holding one of his marbles in his hand tossing it up and down. I looked down to the white sand at my feet and spotted his blue and yellow bomber dug in deep.

"I'll fix you, you son of a hoodlum," I said and stuck the marble in my pocket. Hal jumped up and came tearing at me. I turned heel and ran over by Miss Rowell. I took the bomber out and flipped it up in the air smiling at him. He stopped at the monkey bars and stood scowling at me.

When recess was over I stayed out of Hal's way when we stopped at the water fountain and restrooms.

"Susan and I saw Hal bean you with that marble," Patty said.

"Yeah, ain't it a beauty," I said pulling it out of my pocket to show her.

"You kept his marble? What are you, crazy or something? First you feel sorry for him, and then you take his marble. He'll get you back for sure Cally," Patty warned.

"He don't scare me; besides, somebody's got to let them Peterson's know they can't go around treatin' people like they do," I said.

"That'll be the day when anybody, especially a kid teaches Hal's daddy anything," Patty laughed. Then she changed the subject, "Hey, by the way, did you ask your mom yet if I can spend the night tonight?"

"Yeah, I almost forgot to tell you. Mom is going to call your mom and set it up, and guess what! Bud's getting his car tonight. Dad and Jack Jackson are going down and change some kind of papers today and it will be Bud's."

"Come on girls. Hurry along. The rest of the class is already at the room," Miss Rowell interrupted.

After school Patty and I were both disappointed when her mom picked her up. Patty's grandfather was down with his back again, so the Boyds were going to Jacksonville to spend Thanksgiving with her grandparents.

Mom came and we stopped off at Setzer's to get our Thanksgiving turkey. Bud had one all picked out for us. It was a beauty, 25 lbs. Bud and Larry were busy bagging groceries when we came to the checkouts.

"I get off at five tonight Mom," Bud said, filling our bags up.

"Good," Mom said, "You should be home about the same time your dad and Jack get there."

"They got the title changed?" Bud asked. Mom smiled and nodded. Her green eyes sparkled as she watched Bud's sigh of relief and a big grin appear on his worried face.

"Do you mind if Larry comes for supper?" Bud asked.

"Always room for Larry, Buddy," Mom said. My night wasn't going to be completely ruined after all I thought.

Dad and Jack Jackson showed up just after Bud and Larry, just like Mom had said. We all walked out to the shed to raise up the galloping ghost from its resting-place. Jack Jackson swung the big wooden doors open. "Don't forget the battery in her is getting pretty old. You might want to go check on a new one before you go drivin' her too much," Jack Jackson said handing Bud the two silver keys.

"Yes Sir, I will, first thing tomorrow morning," Bud said. He looked proud as our old dog Fluffy did when she had her new pups.

"Hop in," he told Mom and Dad, "You get first ride." Lynn and I chased after them waving as the red tail-lights cast a pinkish red glow in the early evening dusk.

It wasn't very long before round headlights flashed up the drive. Me, Lynn and Kate could hardly wait for the car to come to a stop. We rushed to open the doors.

"Hold on there, gals," Dad said as the big gray door creaked open. "We're going to have supper; then you all can have your ride."

"But Dad," Kate said.

"No buts. Supper will be ruined if we don't get to it. Buddy wants to show Larry's dad the car later, so you can all go into town with them. I'll even spring for icecream," Dad said.

"We get to go cruisin' with Bud and Larry," I said.

"Great," Larry mumbled.

"Dad?" Bud said.

"It will be after seven by the time supper is over and dishes are cleaned. You can have the girls home by nine and then you and Larry can go about your business," Dad said.

"Yes sir, Bud answered. Bud and Larry rolled their eyes and didn't seem too happy about that arrangement.

"You promised them, Bud," Dad said, losing patience.

Supper was a blurr of plate passing and forks moving fast and furious. Afterwards we must have set some kind of record doing dishes. Bud and Larry were trying to help. They were being more of a nuisance hurrying us along so. Mom hollered, "Save the pieces," as Bud clanked a stack of dry dishes into the cupboard. They weren't fooling me any. The sooner we got out the door, the sooner they could bring us girls back home. I could tell there was more on their minds than hanging out with Bud's little sisters for the evening.

Dishes put away and the table wiped, we finished in spite of their help. Bud told Mom and Dad we were leaving and Mom reminded Bud to have us girls home by nine. Bud hurried us out the back door before there were any more hold ups and we all piled in the gray Plymouth, me up front with Bud and Larry, and Kate and Lynn in the back.

"One stop first," Bud said, as he turned the car left instead of right towards town.

"Where we going?" I asked.

"Glorias coming along," Bud answered.

Kate and Lynn giggled. One of them whispered, "First date."

I crossed my arms. "I suppose this means I ride in the back now?"

"I suppose you're right," Bud said smiling in the rear view mirror as he poked me gently with his elbow and whispered, "We'll take that special ride tomorrow Cal. I promise." We turned into the Collier's driveway.

Bud went in to get Gloria, and I crawled in the backseat with a smug Kate and Lynn. Larry turned the key and spun the radio dial. Stations crackled and whistled in and out.

"504 North Boulevard, everything that tastes real fine, that's Johns, Johns, Johns, place to go," came blasting out to the tune of "The Stripper." It was special request night. Patty and I liked to call in and request songs for kids at school-love songs for kids like Tommy Cox and Mary McDouglas, who couldn't stand one another, and goofy songs like "Charlie Brown," for weirdos like Mr. Adams the sixth grade teacher.

The car door opened and Gloria slid in beside Larry. She amazed me how she never looked a mess. Everything was always perfect, like one of those girls on Bandstand. She even smelled good. Probably not "Evening in Paris" from McCrory's five and dime.

I guessed it wasn't so bad bringing her along. I liked her okay and everyone seemed to liven up when she got in the car. Especially Bud. His bad mood from back at the house seemed to be gone.

Just before we got to the stop sign where our road met the river road Bud asked Larry the time. It was seven thirty already.

"Damn, it's going to be too late if we go to town first," Bud said.

"Too late for what?" Kate asked.

Bud stopped the car and turned on the interior light. He pulled out a folded up piece of paper from his pocket. "We're going to make just one more stop before we go to town. You all have to swear right now to keep quiet and wait in the car until Larry and I come back or I'll take you back home," he said.

"I don't like the sound of this. Where are we going?" Kate asked.

Bud handed Kate the note. Lynn and I huddled around Kate to see.

"Bud, this is that paper you found at that old hotel by the river. You're not going back there in the dark are you?" she asked.

Bud was getting pretty aggravated now, "Kate I told you I thought there was something strange about that place. Look at the date and time at the bottom of the page."

"It's todays date and says seven o'clock," she said.

"Right. Something is supposed to happen there tonight and I want to see what it is." Seeing the expression on Kate's face Bud said, "Don't worry. I'll park you by the railroad tracks and Larry and I will run down there, look and come right back. No big deal," Bud assured her.

Well, it was a big deal to Kate, and I can't say I was too keen on the idea either. Kate started yelling about panthers and bob-cats and weirdo two legged animals coming and tearing us to shreds. She said, "All you'll find is a carload of bones and blood when you come back."

I was ready to go home.

"Come on, Kate, it says there on the paper that whatever it was started at seven and it's already after seven thirty now. We could already be there by now if you'd stop your yappin'," Bud said. "I swear we'll just run down and back."

"Then we get ice cream at the Freeze-ette?" she said.

"Right!" The tone of Bud's voice didn't convince me. Bud flipped off the light and turned the galloping ghost onto the river road. Just past the Circus grounds we pulled into a Phillips 66 for gas. Bud handed the attendant two dollars.

A black pick up caught my eye on the other side of the pump.

"Hey Buddy, isn't that the truck we saw down at the boathouse," I said looking out the rear window. My mouth dropped open when I saw skinny Zeke filling up a gas can next to the truck.

"I believe you're right Cally.

"I'm right Bud. That's one of the men that was inside with Isaac," I said, ducking down in the seat.

"He's leaving Cally," Larry said. The truck sped out of the station and onto the river road.

The attendant finished putting the gas in and we headed out.

Just a little ways beyond the station Bud said, "Here's the road," and the car thumped off the blacktop. We bounced along, pieces of gravel hitting the sides of the car as we went. It was blacker than a starless sky with nothing but the headlights and moon to guide us. We came to the swamp that wove down by the tracks. The car rumbled across it on a wooden plank bridge. Larry opened his window and looked out to make sure the wheels didn't get too close to the edge. Bud hung his head out the other side as he steered the car along. The road curved again and in the headlights you could see the railroad tracks coming up ahead. We pulled up along side the tracks just beyond the tunneled road leading to the old hotel. Bud stopped.

"I'll leave the keys," Bud said, "Keep the doors locked and don't open them until we get back."

"No problem!" Kate grouched. Bud and Larry started out and Gloria told them she wanted to come along. Well, if she was going I was too. I didn't want to listen to Kate complain the whole time. So I followed Gloria.

"I don't know Cally, maybe you should stay with Kate and Lynn," Bud said.

"I feel safer with you, Bud. Please let me come.

"Well, whoever's coming come on. Just keep up," Bud said turning and walking away.

It was chilly outside the car. I could see my breath. We ran down the tunneled road. The moss looked ghostly hanging up above. As we got closer we could see lights on at the hotel.

"Whoa!" Larry went down on his backside slipping on the dew covered pine needles.

Rows of cars were parked in an open area down near the river. Another dirt road ran along the river's edge. Men's voices carried through open windows into the night air. Gray and Black shadows moved across the visible side of the front porch and disappeared into the darkness. The four of us moved quickly to the back of the old hotel. It was dark there and felt safe.

"Stay here. I'm gonna' crawl up on the side porch and have a look in that first window there," Bud said. Bud moved slick as a cat stalking a bird. He came back with a jump off the porch scaring the daylights out of us. Gloria slapped a hand over her mouth. There were footsteps on the side porch. Silence. We held our breath. The footsteps went back the other direction.

"Bud, what is it?" Gloria asked.

"It's a friggin' Klan meeting is what it is. The place is crawling with them."

There was a crackling rumble and suddenly the night lit up like the Fourth of July. Footsteps could be heard shuffling around inside the hotel. In the brilliant dancing light shadowy figures with strangely pointed heads loomed across the grounds and into the pine forest. Voices carried from the side of the hotel that was now bathed in what looked like firelight. We quickly gathered close to that side and Bud slowly poked his head around the edge of the building, then jumped quickly back whispering, "It all makes sense now, the poles, the gas and burlap. It's the Klan all right. They're cross burning." Holy Smoke, I thought to myself as I took a peek. "Wow! I wish Patty could see this, she'd absolutely croak," I whispered. Someone jerked me backwards.

"Cally! They'll see you," It was Gloria.

"Maybe we better get out of here. No telling what they'd do to us if they caught us spying on them," Larry said.

"Listen," Bud whispered holding up his hand.

A man's voice silenced the mumblings going on near the burning cross. The voice echoed in the stillness of the fiery night, "AYAK!"

The crowd answered, "AKIA!"

"What the…" Larry said into the night.

The man continued, "For my country and my Klan, our fellow Klansmen and our home…" and they all broke into the Pledge of Allegiance. The gosh darn pledge of allegiance. The one I said every day in school. It seemed a sacrilege as it spewed from his mouth now.

Gloria said, "How dare he talk about 'Justice for all'" By now we were all craning our necks around the corner. I was down on my knees and three pairs of eyes stared out above me. The crowd, all in all, had to be 150 or more. One hundred-fifty ghostly white sheets flapping in the breeze around a burning cross. The speaker stood up on a raised platform behind the podium we had seen the other day inside the hotel. The big silver sword rested against the stand and three flags, American, Confederate and the White one with the cross were held high by hooded figures on either side of the podium.

The speaker shouted, "Brothers of the River Hunt Club Klavern we are gathered here tonight to welcome three new upstanding white Americans to our den. But before their initiation I want you to welcome a man you're all familiar with. Brothers welcome a Klan Kludd himself, Brother Leach, coming all the way from Alabama." Loud cheers exploded from underneath the hoods.

"Brother Leach has come to speak to you about this here atrocity been bilging up around these here parts. I give you Brother Leach!"

Again, the crowd went nuts, yelling and carrying on so. You'd a thought he was the President or something instead of some Klod or Klud or whatever they called him. Brother Leach had the fanciest white sheet of the bunch. All kinds of little gold pins and such that shimmered in the firelight. When he opened his mouth to speak all eyes were glued to him.

He began, "I'm here to tell you good folks tonight, the only hope, the only salvation of the white Protestant gentile in the U.S. of A. today is the United Klans of America." Cheers rang out once again and he continued. Everytime he bellered something the crowd got a little more stirred up.

"We got to protect our own," he said pounding his fist on the podium. Reminded me of something. I couldn't remember. "Wake up!" he said, "We got us a bunch of dictators up in Washington trying to tell us what's good for us. Trying to tell us to go mixing black and white together."

There was a bunch of "Hell No's" from the crowd. He went on, "I say anybody lies with the devil, will die and go to hell without God." With that people started whooping and carrying on.

"What the hell does he think he is, some half-assed preacher or something?" Bud asked.

"He ain't no preacher," Gloria said, "He's a rabble-rousing, hell-fire speaker from the devil."

Brother Leach went on about how cows and horses don't mix, or pigs and dogs. Said it wasn't natural to put black and white children in the same schools, "We must protect our children, not sell them out to a bunch of niggers and nigger lovers, like your good Senator Collier," he pounded again. "If you won't stop it and protect our children then go to niggertown, be one of them, but don't call yourself an American." Leach then pointed out one of the new members and asked, "Tell me, brother, why do you want to be a Klansman?"

The man said, "I got a wife and five kids; I think that's enough reason. I want them to have a country to be raised up in like I was. Nobody forced me to go to school with no nigger. I want them to have them rights."

There was a bunch of "Amens", and Brother Leach told them to pray with him.

"I'll bet they're the ones been sending my Dad all those threats," Gloria said, "Can you believe it? Those thugs are actually praying to God. Shoot, they wouldn't know God unless he came up in a white robe and hood. That's all they understand."

A voice boomed so loud that my heart jumped in my throat. It was the first speaker, the one that introduced the preacher man, "Are you a native-born, white, gentile, American citizen?"

"Yes, replied a voice.

"Do you believe the tenets of the Christian religion?"

"Yes," again.

"Kneel on your right knee Klansmen, One and all. Let us pray."

Silence.

"Bud, this is scary. I want to go home," I told my brother. "Shhh," Bud said.

"Welcome you to citizenship in the Invisible Empire, Knights of the Ku Klux Klan," the one in charge said.

There was cheering and applause, then the leader said, "You may pass on. Forward March."

The three initiates were marched in front of all the other members, who had begun to line up, so as to participate in a very strange handshake as the new members passed by them.

A different voice, but a familiar one said, "This meeting of the brothers of the River Hunt Club is adjourned. Nighthawk and the three new initiates will remain for their instructions. You will perform your first assignment tonight to prove your loyalty to the Klan."

We ducked back behind the hotel. "Bud, what if they see your car when they leave," I began to panic.

Bud put his hand on my arm, "It'll be okay Cally, they'll most likely leave on that dirt road by the river. The other one is out of their way and longer."

We watched in frozen silence until the last taillights were a reddish haze reflecting along the river's edge and disappeared around the bend. There were three or four automobiles left in the grassy parking lot. One by one we crawled up on the side porch. Four men entered the hotel, robes and hoods still on. A fifth man still in his ghostly costume came in off the porch. "Everything ready for us?" one of the men asked the fifth.

"Everything you need is in the boat. There's a spotlight, bottles, and gas in the back bait box. Make sure you cut the engine when you approach the canal," the fifth man said in a muffled voice. I knew where I'd heard it before.

"Come on, boys, time to take care of business," Skinny Zeke told the other four.

"I wish they'd take off those hoods so we could get a good look at them," Larry said.

Gloria said, "Yeah, isn't it funny they have to hide behind white sheets if they are such fine upstanding citizens."

"We better get out of here before they come out," Bud said.

I never ran so fast in my life, but Gloria ran faster. She saw I was falling behind so she grabbed my hand and ran with me. We were just about out of the tunneled road and Bud turned and waited on us to catch up. When we reached the car Larry said, "Hey Bud, car lights are coming from the hotel."

"Holy shit, everybody in the car," Bud said reaching for the handle. "It's locked. Kate open the door!" Bud yelled pounding on the glass. Kate pulled up each of the locks and Bud jerked the door open and shoved me in. I fell into the back seat over Kate's outstretched leg.

"Ouch. Hey that hurt Cally," Kate said sitting up.

"What the heck?" Bud said. "Kate did you have the radio on? The damn car won't start."

"Just for a little bit until it started fading out," Kate said.

"Jese o' Pete," Bud said, "You've run the friggin battery down."

I was watching the car lights approaching the dirt road. "Buddy they're coming," I cried. I had a huge knot in my stomach, and thought I might be sick.

"Lynn, you and Cally get on the floor." Bud said.

"Lynn's asleep," Kate said.

"How can she sleep through all this," Bud yelled starting to panic now. "Wake her up and get her on the floor, and throw that blanket over the two of them. Larry, crawl over the seat and sit next to Kate."

"What?" Kate squeaked. Larry came tumbling over the seat and something hit me in the back of the head.

"Sorry, whoever I just hit with my elbow," Larry said.

"Bud what's happening; do you know what time it is?" Kate complained.

"Shut up Kate," Bud said, "I have to think.

"If you had thought we wouldn't be here," Kate said smartly.

"For crying out loud Kate quit your complaining. That was the Klan down there," Buddy said.

"What?" Kate stammered again.

"Larry, put your arm around Kate," Bud ordered.

"What?" Kate said again.

"Kate you sound like a gosh darn parrot," I said from under the blanket, "What, What, What?

"Bud, it looks like that black truck from the station again and it's stopped at the end of the road. Wait a minute it's coming this way. Shit," Larry said.

"Everybody stay in the car and be quiet," Bud said, "I'm getting out. Just stay quiet, I'm gonna see if he'll give me a jump."

"Be careful Bud," Gloria said her voice shaking. Somebody tucked the blanket around Lynn and me. I was so scared I was afraid they could hear my heart pounding. The car door opened, then shut. I could hear another door shut and a man said, "What are you kids doing way out here?"

Bud was talking now; "Well sir, my buddy and I came out here with our girls. You know."

The man sort of laughed. Then his voice was right next to the car.

"Nobody move; he's looking in the window," Larry whispered.

"This ain't no place to be bringing young girls. You all best get on out of here," the man said.

"Well, I'd like to do that sir, but I think my battery is dead. Car won't start. You wouldn't mind givin' me a jump would you?" Bud said.

"Pull the hood boy. I'll get my truck," was all he said. Larry's voice came in hushed whispers as he filled Kate and Lynn in on what happened. I was more interested in the sounds going on outside.

Metal squeaked and the car rocked a little. An engine started up. Not ours. Lights were inside the car now, flittering through the blanket. Suddenly the door opened and a blast of cool air rushed in. It felt good. It was getting mighty hot down on the floorboards. Someone got in. It was Bud.

"Please start," Bud said. A slow uneven whirring sound jolted the car, then nothing. Again, the same whirring noise.

"Come on galloping ghost," Gloria said, "You can do it."

All at once the engine gave one more whirr and then started.

"Thank you, Jesus," Larry said. Bud gassed it a couple times and opened the door again.

"Thanks a lot. We'll be going home now," Bud told the man outside. The door shut. "Stay on the floor 'til we get out of here," Bud warned.

"It's getting hot under here Bud," Lynn said, now wide awake, "I gotta go to the bathroom."

"Just stay put, he's following us out," Bud said.

"Bud if you think those guys are up to something don't you think we better call the police," Kate asked. "And tell them what?" Bud asked Kate. "That a bunch of kids were watching a Klan meeting and we think they're going to do something? To who and where? We don't know anything. Besides, who do you tell? What if we got that Billy Bob cop that threatened Isaac? No, Larry and I are going to drop you all off and then I think we better go check on Isaac."

"If there's going to be trouble don't you think we should at least tell our parents?" Gloria said, "Bud, I think this is more than we bargained for."

"Maybe later," Bud said, "Why is that guy still behind us? We're almost home." The car slowed and turned slamming Lynn and I into one another. More bruises to add to my shins from the kitchen table I thought as my head hit something again.

"Good, he went on by," Bud said. The car finally came to a stop and the blanket lifted off of Lynn and I. "Hurry up in the house. We'll drop Gloria off and…"

Kaboom! Bud's instructions were interrupted.

Ka-boom! The car felt like it was still moving, and a rumbling shook the night air like thunder.

Ka-Boom!! The sound was deafening. We all jumped out of the car.

Mom and Dad ran out of the house. "Bud!" Mom yelled out to us.

"Look at that," Lynn said pointing to the western sky above and through the trees. The sky was lit up in an orange and red glow. More rumbles surrounded us, and the ground shook beneath us.

"The boathouse!" Bud screamed. He jumped back in his car and Dad and Larry climbed in with him. As the car sped down the drive Dad hollered out the window, "Call the Volunteer Fire Department."

Kate ran in to call, and Mom told Gloria she'd better go with Kate and call her father and let him know she was safe.

I wrapped myself around one side of Mom. Lynn was on her other. We stood clinging to one another staring into the fiery sky.

I don't know how long we stood there watching before we heard the sirens whining off in the distance. Wood crackled in the flames and a nose burning pungent smell hung in the air around us. Mom broke our trance, gathering us in her open arms. "I think we'd better go inside. We can watch from the living room picture window."

I wanted to stay outside. What I'd really wanted was to go with Dad and Bud. I couldn't help myself. I wanted to experience it all, the smells, the sounds, the fury of it. Going inside would somehow be like the end of an exciting movie. Suddenly it's over, the lights come on and none of it was real. This was real and I wanted to remember.

Inside we watched the flaming fingers of the blaze reach upward towards the big dipper, then slowly it turned to a hazy veil of smoke and struggling flame. Probably from the water the firemen were attempting to tame its rage with.

I must have drifted off when the rumbling of an engine roused my droopy eyelids in time to catch a wide chrome bumper of a now silent firetruck under the street light.

Lynn and Kate were curled up on the ends of the sofa. I closed my eyes and hugged the couch back resting my face on my hands. Quiet was good. Quiet was safe. Mom and Gloria's soft whispers floating from the kitchen with smells of freshly brewed coffee, gently lulled me.

When my eyes opened again it was Bud's Plymouth I saw. Not galloping, just ghostly, making its way up the drive through the early morning fog. I wandered into the kitchen with Mom and Gloria and we watched Dad and the boys drag themselves dog tired in the back door. Black soot streaked their faces and clothes. They stooped down and removed ash covered shoes, tossing them on Mom's clean linoleum floor. Each collapsed onto a kitchen chair and we waited for one of them to speak. Mom placed a gentle hand on Dad's shoulder as he leaned back and wiped his black stained hands across his face. Gloria poured three cups of the steaming coffee and we placed the cups in front of them. Bud stared blankly, his red eyes ringed with black dirt. Clean white streaks ran through the soot and down his cheeks from the corners of his eyes.

The quiet was not the calming one like before and I couldn't contain myself any longer. I had to know, "It was the boathouse wasn't it?"

Dad looked at me and took a sip from his cup. "It burnt to the ground. The only thing left is part of the dock down near the water. The rest is nothing but rubble. The firemen tried, but it was just too intense," Dad said.

"What's Isaac going to do? That's his home." Nobody was looking at me. Louder I said, "Where is he? Where did Isaac go?"

Dad closed his eyes and looked down at the table and his voice was slow and grim when he answered, "I'm afraid Mr. Washington was in the boathouse when it burned Cally." A knot filled my throat so tight I thought I'd choke. My knees buckled and Mom grabbed hold of me. I sank to the floor burying my head in Mom's robe. "No" was all I could muster and Dad's voice continued, "The sheriff figures he fell asleep with a cigarette and…"

Bud jumped up, "That's a lie! I told him that's not the way it happened."

Bud was yelling at Dad, the muscles in his neck stretched tight and the veins stuck out.

"Bud!" Dad said, "That's enough. You don't know what happened anymore than we do." Bud shoved the chair out of his way violently spilling coffee all over and left the room, Larry following. Dad called after him and the front door slammed.

Dad ran his hands through his hair and mumbled something I couldn't understand. Mom helped me to my feet as my sobs quieted.

"What's wrong, Will; why did Bud say the sheriff is a liar?" Mom asked, startled by all the fuss.

Throwing his hands up in the air and slamming them back on the table, spilling more coffee, Dad said, "Bud's got some cockin'bull story that the Klan burned down the boathouse. Couldn't come up with anything to back it up and called Sheriff Baines a liar and ranted and raved like he did just now."

"Do you think that's possible, about the Klan I mean?" Mom asked.

"Anything's possible Kathryn, but it's up to the sheriff to find the answers, not some half-crazed kid with a vivid imagination," Dad said.

I left the kitchen. Isaac was dead. Burnt to a crisp and everyone was yelling and carrying on, and it made my head ache. A flash of Isaac on fire screaming ran through my head. I wondered if they found his bones. I tried to shake the thoughts off. Did he wake up or just sleep as the fire stole his life away. I squinted my eyes tight to stop my thinking, but it didn't work. Another face cut through my mind like a sword. A white sheeted face with only black holes for eyes. A ghostly figure holding a big sharp silver sword. White sheets flapping through red and orange flames. I didn't believe the cigarette story either. I had to find Bud.

I looked all around the big white house and checked the shed. Jack Jackson's bees were furious inside their hives. Their buzzing was the only sound to be heard. The morning dew soaked my canvas sneakers. The smell of damp smoke hung in the air. Bud and Larry weren't anywhere to be seen. The Plymouth was still in the shed so I knew they couldn't have gone far. As bad as I wanted to talk to Bud exhaustion was taking a strong hold of me. I went back inside. Bud would have to come home sooner or later. Maybe he'd feel more like talking then. Right now I wanted to sleep and not think anymore.

CHAPTER FOURTEEN

The smells of pumpkin and cinnamon awakened my taste buds and my eyes opened to bright afternoon sunlight. Tomorrow was Thanksgiving and Mom was baking her pies. A tiny black spider twirled the beginning of a new web in the corner. Sleep was good, but not long enough. It didn't take away the terrible things we'd seen the night before. "Isaac," I said as tears blurred my eyes. Here in my room safely tucked under warm blankets it all seemed distant and dreamlike. A nightmare to be sure. My friend, Isaac, just a harmless gentle old man was dead. The boathouse was gone and the evil men who'd done it all were still out there. Now that was a nightmare.

I got up and went to Bud's room. I took a relieved breath. He was sleeping on top of the covers, the soot washed away, and damp, ink black hair rumpled against his pillow. A grimy pair of pants and a sweater was thrown over his desk chair on the other side of his bed. The room smelled of smoke. Something caught my eye on the desk. Something new had been added to the collection of biscuit colored, razor edged arrowheads circling the tipi. A sleek polished turquoise stone the shape of an eye lay next to Bud's ebony Seminole arrowhead. I walked around to get a better look. "Ouch! gosh darn it," I stubbed my toe on the footboard of the bed.

"What you doin' Caily?" Bud said groggily.

I jumped, "Jeez Louise, Bud you nearly gave me a heart attack" I said rubbing my sore toe. Bud looked rested. His face wasn't at all the drawn up and strained, grief stricken face I'd seen earlier. "You okay?" I said studying his face. I guess I just expected his eyes to be all welled up with sorrowful tears. This was very peculiar. It was like his shower had washed away all his anger and grief right down the drain.

"I'm fine," he said smiling of all things.

"Fine!" I said, feeling my neck burn with anger. "Our good friend Isaac's body is fish food and your fine?" I asked angered and disappointed at his coolness.

"Shut the door Cally. I've got something to tell you," Bud said.

Shutting the door and walking back to Bud's bedside he said, "The only reason I'm telling you this is because you've been really cool about not saying anything to Mom and Dad about all that's happened lately. And, besides that, I don't want you to end up some emotionally scarred, psychotic little kid picturing poor Isaac burnt to a crisp."

Something was very strange here. Bud was joking. "So spill it already," I said sitting down on the bed.

Bud looked at me square in the eyes and whispered, "Isaac's not dead."

"What do you mean he's not dead!" I yelled.

"Shhh," Bud said putting his hand over my mouth, which he held there while he went on, "When Larry and I ran out earlier we went to the boathouse, or what used to be the boathouse. We were sitting there on what's left of the dock staring into the canal. Then all of a sudden rippling in the water, his dark face reflecting up at us was Isaac." I had quit squirming and Bud slowly pulled his hand away. "I mean to tell you we thought we'd just seen one of Jack Jackson's ghosts," Bud said with a nervous laugh. "Me and Larry nearly fell in the river trying to get away. Isaac grabbed hold of us before we took the plunge and jerked us backwards. Cally I've never been so glad to see a ghost in my life. Isaac is alive." Bud was smiling but his eyes were damp. A wave of peacefulness came over me and I wanted to shout out loud, "halleluja!"

"Anyways," Bud said wiping his eyes, "Isaac led us over behind the stand of oaks by the water so as to stay hidden from any passersby, and told us what happened. He saw the whole thing Cally. He was gigging frogs off in the cattail pond beyond the boathouse when he heard a boat engine approaching, then it cut off. He started up to the clearing and saw four men wearing white robes and hoods hunched down in the boat. Two of them got out on the dock with sticks of dynamite in their hands and laid them on the window ledges, lit them and ran back to the boat. The other two threw bottles with lit up rags in them into the dock area. They turned the motor back on and took off before all hell broke loose." My mind raced with the images. It was like having one of them old timey movies flickering through my head.

Bud continued, "When the men were gone Isaac watched explosion after explosion destroy his home. He knew the firemen's hoses were helpless against all that power. Half scared to death he went back down to the pond and hid amongst the cattails and brush. At some point Isaac fell asleep and the next thing he knew he awoke to Larry and me talking."

"So you took him to the sheriff right? And, told him everything, right? Bud?"

"No Cally, he wouldn't hear of it. Isaac said it'd be a colored man's word against the Klan. They'd get him for sure. Larry and I wanted to take him to Ocala to find his family, but he wouldn't go there either. He's stubborn as they come. He's got it in his head he's got to stay here and find a way to catch them devils. Says he can't let them get away with burning up all those people's boats, let alone his home."

"Well what's he going to do Bud? He can't hide out in that pond forever?"

Bud's eyes drew close and he set his mouth tight as he spoke, "This is the part you have to give your solemn oath of secrecy to Cally. I mean it, not a word to anyone."

I crossed my heart and hoped to die if I talked, then spit on my hand and stuck it out for Bud to shake. Spittin' was a sure sign of loyalty.

"Isaac's hiding out at that old cabin across the field. The one with that big green lizard that nearly scared Kate and Gloria to death. Larry's going to bring out an old kerosene heater to keep Isaac warm at night and I'll take him that gas camp stove to cook on. He can stay there until we find evidence to put those guys away. Isaac has it all figured out. Isaac said the one guy dropped a stick of dynamite by the bushes. Isaac grabbed it up before the explosion. Larry and I need to go back to that old haunted hotel and snoop around. There's got to something there we can use against them. Maybe in that motor boat."

"I'll help you Bud," I said.

"No! This time you can't go down there Cally. It's too dangerous. That one guy Zeke drove his black pickup by the fire a couple times last night." Bud shook his head, "Can't take no chances."

"Just when things are getting real excitin'," I said.

"I'll tell you what Cal, you keep quiet and help me take food to Isaac and I'll start teaching you how to drive the galloping ghost on the dirt road runs by the cabin," Bud promised. I quickly agreed.

Bud made me swear one more time to let him take care of it and stay out of this mess. I swore on my grandmother's grave, but Bud reminded me our grandmother was alive and well in Atlanta. I swore and we shook on it. Bud wouldn't let me spit this time.

CHAPTER FIFTEEN

Thanksgiving came with a shiver. Dad piled logs in the fireplace to take the chill off the house. The turkey was in the oven and the scent of sage dressing got my saliva glands working. Mom invited the Senator and Gloria for dinner and they accepted. As usual it was a feast beyond comparison. Roast turkey and dressing, cranberries, sweet potatoes with pecans, corn pudding and trays of sliced up cheese, pickles and such. Mom topped it all off with homemade apple cinnamon and pumpkin pies. The senator swore he'd never had such a fine meal, not even at the White House.

After we ate, the adults retired to the living room for conversation and us kids gathered up a small feast for Isaac. Bud had to tell the girls when Kate got suspicious of what Bud and I was doing with the leftovers. Strangely for Kate, she didn't throw one of her tizzies and she helped.

Bud and I delivered the small feast and Isaac was real grateful. He gobbled down every last morsel. We took him an old army blanket from the attic, an extra pillow we used for company and a can opener. Bud and Larry were to buy some canned goods at Setzers. I hated to leave Isaac there alone, but Bud said we had just enough daylight left for my first driving lesson before we had to get on back home.

Bud told me to sit alongside him in the ghost while he showed me all the gears and such. I never realized there was so much work involved in driving. Bud switched places with me after I caught on real good to gears one, two, three, and reverse and had me practice how to push the pedals. In order to reach them I had to sit on the edge of the seat, but then I had a time seeing over the steering wheel. Bud turned the key and told me to push on the clutch and push the gear. A most terrible grinding came out from underneath us. Bud yelled to push the pedal. I was so scared I let go of everything and the ghost took a giant lurch forward and died. I could hear hooting and laughing coming from inside the cabin. Surprisingly Bud stayed pretty cool and we tried again. This time I jerked and lurched but I kept her going, until I nearly went in the ditch across the road. That was the end of my first lesson.

When we returned home, Bud went up and got his baseball card collection to show the Senator. The Senator seemed like a real regular guy. Dad had to admit later when Gloria and her father left that for a politician he was a decent man. The day was pretty uneventful, which, considering the last couple of days, was certainly something to be thankful for. The only tense moment came when Mom was heating up leftovers and swore there was more turkey left than there was. "Next year we better get a bigger bird," she said.

CHAPTER SIXTEEN

Saturday was a red-letter day. Next to Christmas this particular Saturday was the day every kid in DeLeon waited for all year long. It was the day of the DeLeon Christmas parade, which was the signal for the start of the holidays. All the decorations would be up in the store windows and Santa Clauses would be ringing their bells on every corner collecting money in the red Salvation Army pails. People would smile at one another and Christmas carols would play from speakers along the boulevard. The only thing missing would be snow.

Before breakfast Dad was reading the paper at the kitchen table. "Says here there's a memorial service Sunday at the Calvary Baptist church for Isaac Washington. It's amazing how little we knew about the man. Says here he was a life long member of the congregation. He loved to fish and it mentions something about his being the caretaker of the cemetery." Dad shook his head; "It's a damn shame that's what it is. A little further down here it says after a short investigation the sheriff and the owner of the boathouse agreed it was an accident."

Bud winked at me. We hurried through breakfast so we could get downtown and find a good parking spot before the parade began at ten o'clock. We wanted a front row seat because Senator Collier would be riding in one of the cars and Gloria was riding with him. This was her last day home before returning to school until Christmas break. Bud was absolutely gloomy about it.

It was a sunny day and the brass dome on the courthouse glistened. It was the first thing anyone saw when they were coming into town. Besides the bell tower at the college the courthouse was the tallest building in town.

Mom, Dad, Kate and Lynn found a spot under a magnolia tree for shade and spread out their blanket. Bud and me went on down in front of the Masonic temple next to the bridge crossing Raccoon Creek. The parade always started on the other side of the bridge in front of the college. The town looked just like one of those picture postcards all decorated up. The home of the president of the college was gorgeous with green ropes of garland wrapped around the columns decorated with red velvet bows. Big clay pots filled with bright red poinsettias ran all along the veranda and down the brick walk.

The fire station whistle blasted signaling the beginning of the parade. Over the bridge came float after float. The DeLeon High band played Rudolph and the majorettes wore little reindeer antlers on their heads. One pretty hefty reindeer dropped her baton, and when she bent to pick it up, I winced waiting for green and gold sequins to explode all over the pavement. Next came the politicians waving pamphlets and throwing candy from convertibles. Gloria and her dad were the first. Bud's face reddened, then flashed a proud grin as Gloria hollered out, "Hey Bud," and threw me a handful of red peppermint candies. She looked beautiful as usual and Bud's eyes followed the red sports car wonderstruck.

Some boys from school came by in their Cub Scout uniforms. I laughed as Tommy Cox, out of step had to keep skipping to stay in time.

Finally, we spotted the red hat coming over the bridge. A huge red and white crepe paper float with little elves sitting in front of a big white sleigh held what I came to see. Perched there high in the sleigh sat what I thought to be the best Santa DeLeon had seen as long as I could remember. He had big plump rosy cheeks and a long full white beard that no way wasn't real.

A jazzed up version of "Here Comes Santa Claus" followed Santa's float. Dozens of brown faces framed in red Santa hats marched by. Not the stiff serious marching of the other bands ahead of them, these marchers strutted, bobbing back and forth, gyrating to the beat of the drummers following behind them. It was the Bethune-Cookman College band. People looked forward to hearing them every year. They'd won all kinds of contests up state. The crowd, including Bud and myself, clapped to the rhythms. My clapping stopped directly upon looking beyond the last of the drummers at the top of the bridge. "Oh my gosh! Bud! What on God's green earth are they doing here?" I said staring in disbelief. Bud grasped my shoulder and I watched in silent horror and loathing as the first row of pointed white hoods rose into view. Row by row of horses mounted with white robed riders clopped across the bridge, hoods hiding their identities. I gulped in a deep breath not realizing I had been holding it, and then I saw it. A pearly white and black snakeskin boot slipped in a brass stirrup passed in front of me. On its side was an empty black crevice where a turquoise stone once had been. My stomach turned. I was suddenly grabbing Bud by his sleeve not taking my eyes off the boot. "Where did you find it?" I found myself repeating over and over.

Bud yelled, "Cally what the devils got into you? Where did I find what?"

"The stone," I said, "The turquoise stone. The one in your room with the arrowheads."

Bud looked mystified, and then a look of understanding came over him. "That turquoise stone on my desk? I found it lying on the dock the night of the fire."

I grabbed his hand and pulled him along the parade route pointing at Roy Peterson's boot from the sidewalk.

"Cally what are you pointing at? You're acting like a lunatic!" Bud screamed in my face.

Now in complete control of my senses I took a deep breath and said directly into Bud's befuddled stare, "That stone fell out of Roy Peterson's boot when he and those other men burned up the boathouse. I saw him wearing those snakeskin boots up at the river grocery. I remember them because of the blue stone that looked like snake eyes. That same stone is missing out of the boot, and you have it."

"Cally, do you realize what you're saying? What we have here is our first solid piece of evidence connecting Roy Peterson and the Klan to the fire. We've got to tell Isaac. Larry and I have got to get down to that hotel. The stone is good, but not enough."

There were firecrackers or something down the route and the men dressed in Civil War costumes fired off their muskets. The Klan was the last of the parade. For the life of me I couldn't figure out how come they were out in public, in broad daylight, let alone in the Christmas parade. So much for Christmas cheer.

A crowd was gathering down at the south end of the boulevard. People were running and sirens were blasting. The parade had stopped. Santa Claus crawled off his float and was running towards all the commotion. The closer we got it was pretty clear the ruckus wasn't part of the festivities. Bud stopped a red-faced man who was running towards us. The man's eyes were wild and perspiration covered his face. "What's all the noise about?" Bud asked.

"The senators been shot," he said breathlessly as he kept moving, his beige trenchcoat flapping around his trousers. Bud and I broke into a run. I spotted Mom, and Dad in the crowd. There were all kinds of people around the red convertible. Gloria was crying cradling her father in her arms. He wasn't dead because his eyes were open and he was talking. A policeman suddenly grabbed hold of me and told me and Bud and the others around us to get back on the sidewalk and make room for the ambulance.

A chubby baldheaded man was telling the police officer, "I heard two shots. One hit the senator and Lord knows where the other went. I just hit the pavement. Didn't see nobody."

"The worlds going to hell in a hand basket," a white-haired old woman said clutching her purse close to her chest.

"Did anyone see the gunman?" the officer asked sounding kind of annoyed.

A small woman not much taller than myself and holding the hand of a little boy with round dark eyes walked up to the officer. "I think I may have seen something," she said in a voice just as tiny as she was. She sounded like one of those Munchkins out of Wizard of Oz. That's what she looked and sounded like, a Munchkin. The police officer took her off to the side.

A siren blasted. The ambulance, its red lights flashing inched through the crowd. People scattered to the curb. I'd lost Bud. Then I spotted him with Gloria. She didn't seem to see anyone except her daddy.

A Sun News photographer was taking pictures of Bud, Gloria and Senator Collier. The ambulance men yelled at the photographer to get out of the way. He kept snapping his camera. The policeman shoved him.

A firm hand touched my arm. It was Dad. "Come on along, Cally. We need to get out of the way here."

I pulled away. Dad said, "Looks like the Senator and Gloria are going to be okay. They're in good hands now Cally. I'm sure Bud will fill us in later. There's nothing we can do here except get in the way." Dad moved his arm around me leading me away, "Come on Honey, let's go home," he said softly.

Part of me wanted to go home where it was safe, but part of me was pulled in and swallowed up by the entire goings on. It was like watching a horror movie through the spaces between my fingers. I was afraid to see, but I just couldn't help myself.

Later at home I had to go to bed before Bud came. I was glad Lynn was there beside me. It was a long time before I could shut my mind to what I had seen.

CHAPTER SEVENTEEN

For a Sunday morning the house was awful quiet. Downstairs Dad was grumbling to himself looking through the kitchen cupboards, "Cally, where's your Mom keep the coffee?"

"Over in the coffee canister," I said. "I knew that," he smiled, giving me his silly wrinkled up nose grin.

As he scooped the coffee into the percolator filter I asked where Mom was.

"I told her to stay in bed. She was up late with Gloria."

"Gloria's here? We told the Senator she could stay with us until he gets out of the hospital," Dad explained.

"I thought she was supposed to go back to school today," I said.

"She's too upset to leave her father right now. He's going to call the school and explain what's happened."

"Sounds like the Senator is doing pretty good for getting shot," I said.

"The bullet hit his arm and fractured the bone. He's a lucky man. Just a couple inches more and it could have been a real tragedy," Dad told me.

"They catch who did it?" I asked. Dad handed me the Sun News off the kitchen counter. 'Senator Collier Shot-Gunman Still at Large' was the headline. My eyes dropped to the big color photo. "Buddy? Dad, Bud's on the front page with the senator and Gloria. The caption read, 'Gloria Collier and male friend console her father, Senator Eugene M. Collier, shot during DeLeon Christmas parade.

"Cally, you hungry? How about some pancakes?" Dad said.

"Sure," I said.

Dad set two of the biggest pancakes in front of me.

"Cool! This one on top looks like a map of the United States," I said. Its edges were all out of whack, nothing like the nice round ones Mom made. I looked down at my plate and up at Dad.

"Just eat it, you can practice your geography while you eat," Dad said with a scowl, waving the spatula in my face. I had eaten most of the southeast when from the corner of my eye I caught a glimpse of something out the kitchen window.

"Dad, there's a man standing out in the side yard," I said starting to get up from the table.

Sit down, sit down Cally girl. It's just that security fella the Senator hired to keep an eye on Gloria.

I gobbled up the rest of the U.S.A. and checked the clock. It was too late to go to Sunday school and I was fairly sure we wouldn't make church being as nobody was stirrin' yet. I'd be willing to bet that old Clara Webb's mouth would be yappin' this morning at church after seeing Buddy in the paper.

After I finished I decided to go outside and check out the security man. I tried to strike up a conversation with him. He stared into space pretending like he was listening, saying yeah, or nodding his head once in a while, but I knew he wasn't paying me no mind. He proved to be pretty uninteresting for a rent a cop, so I went back inside.

Everyone else was up now. Out in the kitchen Kate and Lynn were making up a bunch of sandwiches.

"Somebody going on a picnic?" I asked.

Kate said, "We're going to drop Gloria off at the hospital, then go with Mom and Dad to the new house to work." She slapped my hand away from a bologna and cheese, "The sandwiches are lunch," she said, giving me one of her looks. Bud had the phone receiver cradled in his hands, his back turned to us trying to be inconspicuous, "We'll have to go tonight, it can't wait any longer," he said to whoever was on the other end.

I sat down at the table resting my chin in my hands and listened.

"No kidding?" he said twisting the cord around his fingers, "Old Tyson was there too? Arrested them? I'm telling you Larry we've got to go tonight. I'd do it now but I've got to help Dad this afternoon. It'll be better if it's dark anyways. We'll take the ghost. Your red car's too noticeable."

"You kids about ready?" Dad said, the floor creaking under his work boots in the hallway.

"Dad's coming, be here at seven. Bye," Bud hung up.

"Where you got to go Bud?" I asked.

"You going somewhere?" Dad asked Bud as he came in the kitchen.

"That was Larry we're doing something tonight, not now," Bud said, giving me such a look.

Something big was up and I was determined to find out what it was.

Bud told us part of the phone conversation as we drove to the hospital. "Seems the colored folks had their service for Isaac and afterwards a bunch of them including Isaac's fishing buddy, Tyson, burnt up an old scarecrow dressed in white hood and robe at the courthouse. They all carried signs written up in blood red paint that said things like, 'hooded murderers', and 'justice for all' on them." Bud laughed as he added, "The ones the police could catch, including Tyson didn't make the arrests any too easy. I guess Tyson just sat there, all 300 pounds of him and it took three policemen to carry him off."

"Larry and Bill watched the whole thing from their church parking lot across the street, along with a bunch of their shocked Southern Baptist congregation."

I tried my darndest the rest of the day to find out what was going on at seven o'clock, but Bud was as tight-lipped as a stubborn Kate could be. He did tell me while we were hauling a bunch of scrap back to burn in an old pit Dad dug, that it had something to do with Isaac, which I had already figured. He wouldn't say another word and told me to quit pestering him.

Gloria was a little perkier when we picked her up later. Senator Collier was going to be released in a couple days. Gloria said on the ride home, "The police think they have a lead on who shot my father."

"The Munchkin," I said outloud. Kate choked on a swig of her bottle of soda pop, "A Munchkin? A Munchkin shot the Senator?" She said laughing in between coughs.

"No!" I told her, "The little woman with the big eyed little boy at the parade. She said she saw something when Gloria's daddy got shot. She looked like a munchkin."

"There she goes again, everybody looks like a movie actor or a cartoon character. Now it's Munchkins," Kate went into another fit of laughter, which riled me to no end.

Mom said sharply, "Kate, there isn't anything funny about any of this, and for your information I recall reading in the paper that one of the women staying out at the circus grounds had given a description of a suspect. The paper described her as one of the 'little people' from the circus." This only made Kate double up more trying to contain herself.

"Lions and tigers and munchkins, oh no," Lynn whispered only loud enough for us in the back to hear. Kate was in fits now.

"It's bears not munchkins!" I said right in Lynn's ear.

"Cally!" Dad said, "Hursh!"

Jack Jackson's car was sitting in the driveway when we pulled in. As soon as Dad cut the engine Mr. Jackson sauntered up to Dad's car window. "Looks like ya'll been hard at it today," he said taking off his Caterpillar Hat and scratching his head. "Thought I'd better stop by and warn you one of them lions is running around loose from up to the circus grounds. Keeper forgot to latch the door or something after their evening feed and ole' Brutus escaped."

I thought, oh my gosh, my alarm clock. There was dead silence in the car. Jack Jackson went on, "The Sheriff, some of the circus people and a few of us locals are out tracking him. You folks just be real careful if you're out tonight." Flopping his cap back on his head he said, "I best be getting back with the others. If you see anything Will just call the Sheriff's office."

With that Dad thanked Jack Jackson for the information and the burly giant walked back to his car and left.

"Well, you heard him, everyone get on in the house," Dad said as we got out of the car. Kate's head was turning like the hoot owl sat outside my window at night. She nearly ran over poor Gloria trying to get in the house before something jumped out and got her. Dad told Bud if he was planning on going out he best stick to town, "They'll most likely have old Brutus locked up safely in his cage by then with Jack on his trail," Dad laughed, "But no sense in being foolish."

It was seven o'clock when Larry showed up, right on schedule. He and Bud went out on the glassed in porch and shut the doors. Kate and Gloria asked Dad if they could sit out on the front porch a while. He said as long as they stayed up on under the light it would be all right. I decided to join them. They stopped their conversation as soon as I stepped outside. Kate snipped at me to go back inside. So, I did what any normal little sister would do and went back inside, then upstairs to the bedroom and carefully opened the window that overlooked the area where they were sitting below.

Gloria was saying, "I think we should tell your parents what we know Kate. Those animals think they've killed Isaac and they've tried to kill my father. Larry and Bud could be in grave danger."

"Bud said they need more evidence or nobody will believe them," Kate said. "I don't know what to do, Gloria. I'm scared for Bud."

"Let's make an agreement. If they don't find anything at the hotel tonight then I say we tell what we know and take our chances. It's just too risky," Gloria told Kate.

So that was it. I shut the window and went to the closet and grabbed my jacket.

Downstairs Lynn was glued to Davy Crockett on Walt Disney. Mom and Dad, tired from working on the house, were asleep in their chairs. Dad's mouth was opened wide and his eyelids were slightly parted. He was just getting revved up. Pretty soon Lynn would have to turn up the volume to hear over his snoring.

Opening the back door, Gloria's guard was no where in sight so I made a mad dash across the back yard. The shed doors squeaked as I pulled them open. Remembering old Brutus I quickly closed them behind me. I heard the back door to the house shut and Larry and Bud's voices. Opening the Plymouth door I crawled in the back seat covering myself with the army blanket. The shed doors swung open and my nose was beginning to itch when Bud and Larry opened the car doors and climbed in. Lord, don't let me sneeze, I thought pinching my nose between my thumb and finger. The sensation passed.

"We'll stop by the cabin and check on Isaac on the way," Bud said.

"I sure hope none of those goons are down by the river when we get there," Larry said.

"If we see anybody we'll just have to wait and go back a little later," Bud told him.

Larry turned on the radio. Good, now I can breath normal, I thought.

It feels mighty peculiar when a body's moving and can't see where it's going. Bud hit every bump and pothole as we moved down the road. I felt the car turn and my nose nearly met the floorboards. The car started shaking so hard it felt like every nut and bolt was popping loose. We were on the washboard road leading to the cabin. The car stopped. Both doors opened and Larry and Bud got out. Tossing the blanket off my head I gulped in some air. A little drip of sweat ran from my forehead down my nose and plopped to the floor. Voices came towards the car. Isaac's deep smoky one was telling them he'd be just fine and said, "I ain't gonna let you boys go down there by yourselves. I'll just come along and wait in the car; keep an eye on things whilst you all look around."

They piled in, while Buddy grumbled, "I don't like this, not one bit."

"Well now, Buddy boy. This here is real nice," Isaac said sliding across the wide seat. "Real fine piece of machinery," he said. I could picture his wide cocoa eyes and his big warm grin. Isaac asked, "So what's that you say? Tyson went to the pokie over all this? Old fool, I should've told him I hadn't met my maker yet. Lawd, I hope no harm comes to him down in that jail."

"My daddy said they probably just took them down there to calm them down. Probably let Tyson out already. He's just an old man," Larry tried to assure Isaac.

We were back on the paved road and I was mighty grateful. My bones still felt like they were all jostled up inside. It was like getting off the roller coaster at the carnival. My stomach wasn't feeling too good either. Lord don't let me throw up. I did that sometimes on vacation riding in the backseat. We'd get to that one little town up in the Smokies and everytime I'd get there, barf. Then I'd be fine the rest of the trip. I was starting to feel a little better now.

The car was turning again. It had to be the old dirt river road. Pieces of gravel chinked inside the tire wells.

"Looks pretty deserted so far," Bud said as the car slowed. Click.

"What did you turn the lights out for? It's blacker out here than the ace of spades," Larry said.

"I don't want to advertise our arrival if there is anybody out here," Bud told him.

I was beginning to wish I'd stayed home. All I'd have to do is get up and show my face and Bud would turn around. He'd be madder than all get out though. The car stopped. Somebody opened their window and the crickets were down right deafening. It was getting hotter than an August afternoon under the blanket. If they just left the window open maybe it would cool off before I passed out.

"Look over yonder, floatin' in the river. It's that motor boat brought them men to burn up my place," Isaac said.

"Stay in the car Isaac and we'll go check it out," Bud said as the doors to the Plymouth opened then shut again. I stuck my head out for just a second and took in a deep breath. Then waited, Isaac and me. It was comforting to know he was there even if he didn't know I was. Except for the crickets rubbing their legs together the night was quiet. Every once in a while I could hear a bob-white up in one of the pines twittering out its name Bob-white, Bob-white. Isaac started tapping a nervous finger on the front seat.

"What the..." Isaac's voice whispered, then the car door opened and Isaac jumped.

"You!" a voice growled. I caught a flash of light against Isaac's door. The voice was yelling to someone, "Well, looky here what I got."

Panic ran through me like a cold chill. There was no mistaking it. I was listening to the voice of skinny Zeke. I had no spit to swallow.

Zeke's voice said, "I told him I seen some ghostly grey thing in my headlights. If I didn't know better I say what I'm looking at is a dead man. A real honest to goodness ghost." He started yelling again, "Hurry it up and get over here with them boys Roy. You won't believe what I got here!"

My body started shaking underneath the blanket. "Leave them boys be," Isaac warned, "I'm what you want. Don't be doing them no harm."

There was movement across the front seat then a skin to skin slapping sound, "We'll let you know what we want nigger," Zeke said.

"You okay Isaac," came Bud's breathless voice outside the car.

Roy Peterson's said, "Caught these two messing around the boat Zeke. This one here had this stick of dynamite tucked under his jacket."

"Better be careful boy. They'll be picking up little pieces from here to Lake County," Zeke laughed an evil laugh, then he said, "Hey boy! Don't I know you? Hell yes I do. It's that kid I told you about Roy. The one parked out by the tracks with the dead battery. Then later on that same night I seen this here car up to the boathouse the night of the fire.

"Well now, let me get a better look here," Roy Peterson said…."I'll be damned. I'll tell you what we got here. We got us an honest to goodness celebrity. Don't you read the paper? This here's the boy in the newspaper this morning with that nigger lovin' senator." Now his voice took on a real mean tone, "We got us some real trouble. We got a nigger supposed to be dead and two boys snooping around here looking for something. What might that be boy!" Something slammed up against the car. Then came a low mournful groan and Bud called out Larry's name.

"Daddy don't!" came a voice I knew well. Darned if it wasn't Hal Peterson out there with his Daddy. There was some more slapping around and Hal hollered and Roy Peterson warned, "If I want any lip out of you Son I'll ask. Now go on, get back in the truck! Go on Boy!"

"We need to take a little ride," Zeke said, "And I know just where to. I warned that nigger I'd put him there and now I'm gonna keep my word."

There was a clinking sound, "Take my keys and go back up with your boy and get my truck. I'll drive Mr. celebrities car and you follow us," Zeke said.

There was a lot of scuffling and somebody sort of fell into the back seat. Zeke ordered Bud to give him his keys. It was Bud reaching with the keys from the back. He was so close I could touch him. I didn't dare move. Oh Bud.

"Don't get brave back there. I've got my lugar pointed in your friends bruised belly," Zeke threatened Buddy.

My shaking came in waves and I was so cold. The blanket seemed to be ice not wool. Suddenly something about the size of a foot was tapping against my leg. The blanket lifted and dropped back down. I moved the blanket from my face and turned my eyes towards Bud's horrified face. His hand motioned downward and I covered back up.

Nobody spoke. The silence was nauseating. There were a couple more moans from the front seat.

"My friend's hurt real bad," Bud's voice sounded hopeless.

"Shut up kid, nobody told you to go poking your nose in around here," Zeke said.

It was no longer sweat dampening my face now. My eyes kept filling up as fast as they emptied. I couldn't stop it anymore than I could stop my trembling. The salty overflow ran into my mouth. My throat felt tight and hurt holding back my sobs.

"You won't get away with this. You can't go around terrorizing, blowing up and shooting people," Bud yelled.

Zeke hooted a low down devilish laugh; "They have to catch us first. You're wrong boy, dead wrong. We brothers stick together. The KKK is on the side of right. Hell boy, we are the law around here."

"Whose law? Not Sheriff Baine's or Senator Collier's," Bud said, "You're crazy fanatics. You're going to fry for sure if you do anything to us."

"You talk too much, Celebrity. Now shut that smart mouth before I reach this here gun back and shut it for you. Be like your nigger there. He's learned real good to respect us and keep his mouth shut," Zeke spouted.

"Quit calling him that, and he ain't mine. He don't belong to nobody especially the likes of you," Bud said.

"I said to shut your mouth boy, I won't miss my target this time like I did yesterday," Zeke threatened.

"It was you shot the Senator!" Bud cried.

"Yeah, and it don't matter none to me if I do you now or later," Zeke roared as the key turned to start the grey ghost's engine.

The road was smooth now. I hadn't noticed when we turned onto the paved road. It wasn't long before the car dipped and pulled off the road. I could hear another vehicle pulling in too.

The doors opened. "Umph!" Larry gasped.

"Get out!" Zeke ordered.

"You didn't have to hit him again," Bud said.

"You know I've heard about enough of your mouth, get on out of there now," Zeke told Bud.

There was a lot of stumbling around outside and the two men shouted out orders. The voices grew distant from the car. I waited. My hands felt clammy as I wiped my sweat covered face. It took every last ounce of strength I had as I pulled my stiff aching body up off the floorboards and peered out the window. Grave markers in ghostly moonlight poked up out of the ground. We were in the old colored cemetery. Larry stumbled along behind Roy Peterson who was carrying a big circle of rope draped over his shoulder. Skinny Zeke forced Larry and Isaac along poking his gun at them. Peterson stopped under a big oak near the spot where Patty and I had seen the grave robbers Halloween night. He dropped the coiled rope to the ground holding on to one end, looping and knotting it, drawing it tight. Looking upward to the outstretched limbs he heaped the rope up. Apparently missing his target he did it again.

Larry clutched his stomach and slumped to his knees. My muscles had quit twitching so much, but my insides were all a quiver. An uncomfortable clamminess washed over me and my cheeks stung from dried tears. Suddenly the interior light flickered on and Hal Peterson said, "You!"

I turned just as he was about to crawl back out of the ghost. A wave of fear and excitement took hold of me and I moved like a striking rattler across the back seat and caught hold of Hal's head, jerking him back inside the car. The door clicked shut. Feisty as an old bob-cat Hal kicked and flung himself all over the front seat. I just kept hold of him and wrapped my other hand over his big mouth. Everytime he jerked I don't know where my strength came from, but I tightened my grip around his neck and pulled him into the seat's back. "If you just settle down," I said straining, "I'll turn you loose." He kicked some more, then I gave one more jerk and he let out a muffled groan and calmed a little.

"I don't know what you think about all this, and I personally don't care," I said keeping my grip, "but I'll be damned if I'm going to let Skinny Zeke or your daddy hang old Isaac or maybe kill my brother or anybody else for that matter. I can't believe you'd have any part of something like that, but if you don't help me try to stop it you're no better than them." Hal gave a little tug, but I held fast and went on, "If you help me we can stop this before it goes any farther. So far your daddy was only at the scene the night of the fire at the boathouse. It was Zeke done the shooting. You don't want your daddy mixed up in a murder do you?" Hal wasn't moving now. "Well do you?" I asked again. Still no answer. I jerked his head pulling him across the seat. "Look over yonder," I said shoving his face to the glass in time to see his daddy hurl the rope over the oak tree one final time. This time the rope looped over the limb and draped down the other side. Roy Peterson grabbed hold of the noose and pulled it to him. He placed it over Isaac's head. "Look Hal! Look what's happening! You hang a man, any man, colored or white, it's murder just the same." I realized my hand over Hal's mouth was damp. He was crying. I let go and he moved away from the window. I crawled over the seat next to him. I had to move now. "So what's it gonna be Hal?" I asked.

"What can we do?" Hal said wiping his face. "You know anything about driving cars?" I asked him. "I can drive my daddy's pick up," he answered.

"That's all I want to know. You shift and I'll push the pedals and you can help guide my steerin'," I said.

"Are you crazy?" Hal asked looking at me wild eyed.

"I'm crazy enough," I said, as we watched Roy Peterson tying Isaac's hands behind him. Mine were clammy and sweat covered my face.

"Are you with me or not?" I asked him. "If not sit back and stay out of the way." Hearing no response I ordered, "Let's start her up!"

"I hope you know what you're doing," He said as I pushed in the clutch and told him to let me know if I was gonna hit a tree or something. Shaking his head, he moved the gear in place. I turned the key and stepped on the gas. The ghost leaped forward and I just kept pushing harder on the gas. Hal helped me turn the wheel as the car moved forward. Something screeched against the metal and we were facing the group inside the cemetery. The ghost strained and Hal hollered, "Push in the clutch again!" I did and he shifted into second. I let loose of the clutch and gave it more gas. Things were bumping and thumping outside. The tires bounced over Lord only knew what. I could barely see anything. Hal shouted in my ear, "Look out!" A white stone went flying over the top of the hood and slid off the other side. Hal held tight to the dash and me, I just clutched the steering wheel as we were jostled back and forth, tombstones and dirt flying all over. My heart pounded in my chest. I caught a glimpse of Roy Peterson running towards the road. As I turned my head to where he had lit out from I saw the silver of Zeke's lugar pointed at the ghost. Hal ducked and I closed my eyes tight and shoved on the gas. The explosion of a gun firing pierced my ears just as the car came to a rapid stop throwing Hal and myself into the dash.

My head throbbed and I could hear Hal's voice. He sounded far away at first. "Cally are you dead?" he asked.

"No I ain't dead! What did we hit?" I said looking over the dash at the hangin' tree.

All at once the door opened and Bud was pulling me out hugging me to him. He kept saying, "Cally," over and over again. When Hal and I were safely out of the car and I tried to stand on my own, my legs felt like wobbly rubber bands. Larry was sitting up against a tree still holding his middle. Isaac was bent over someone whom I guessed was Zeke, who lay still, sprawled out on the ground. Roy Peterson was nowhere in sight.

"What happened to Zeke?" Hal asked, starting to go towards the still body.

Bud grabbed Hal's shoulder keeping him back and said, "I think he's dead. I can hardly believe it. It all happened so fast." Zeke shot at you and Cally, and old Isaac, hands still tied behind him charged, head down, and rammed right into Zeke from behind. Zeke fell to the ground, "I guess landing on his gun. Anyhow it went off and he hasn't moved." Bud walked over and removed the noose, still wrapped around Isaac's neck and untied his bound hands. "Is he...?" Bud said quietly placing his hand on Isaac's shoulder.

"Lawd I believe so Buddy," Isaac said in a whisper. Buddy turned Zeke over and in the moonlight you could make out the bloodied shirt and the gun lay on the ground where the body had been. I closed my eyes. Bud started to pick up the gun and Isaac yelled out, "No Buddy! Don't touch it. The only fingerprints gonna be on that gun is that devil's." Buddy jumped back. Hal was out at the road. Looking for his daddy I supposed. Roy Peterson wasn't only an evil bully, he was a coward at that, leaving his son and his friend like he did.

"Somebody's got to get to a phone and call Sheriff Baines," Bud said, "Thing is we can't all go. Someone has to stay with the body, and Larry's hurt pretty badly." Turning towards his car he said, "Doesn't look like the ghost will be going anywhere for awhile, so we'll have to foot it."

"I'll go," I said surprising myself.

"Not by yourself," Bud told me.

"I'll go with her," Hal said walking up. He looked so lost.

I smiled and said, "Let's go then." Hal and I broke into a run.

"Be careful Cal. Hurry back!" Buddy called after us as we ran through the cemetery gates. Running along the paved road I had the feeling I wanted to run forever, as far away as my legs would carry me. The further away from the cemetery we got the freer I felt. The moon glistened as we passed the pasture gate. As we approached the grove I could see the Anderson's darkened house. In the far distance I could just make out the Jackson place. Looked like every light in the house was burning.

I told Hal, "There's my house up ahead." Just a little farther now I told myself.

Cally
& Hal

Something rustled through the bushes to my right, along the edge of the grove. It gave me such a start. Probably just an old jack-rabbit I tried to convince myself. There it went again. Whatever it was, was making a real ruckus in there. Seemed to be moving with us. No jack-rabbit made that much noise. Hal looked over at me and we picked up speed. Branches cracked and the thump of footsteps came in behind us. I turned to look towards the sounds, when Hal hollered. I turned back towards him and saw his daddy collaring him by the back of his shirt, and there came the ripping sounds of material shredding.

"Leave him go!" I yelled.

"Cally, just go on! Run!" Hal cried out just before his daddy slapped a hand over his mouth.

"What's this all about boy?" Roy Peterson demanded. "You wouldn't be thinking of turning in your old daddy would you?"

I didn't know what to do. I stood frozen in the middle of the road.

The bushes rustled again. I turned with a start.

RRRoar!

RRRoar!

A stabbing fear ran through my insides to my very core. In the next second, Brutus, with one mighty leap sprang from the darkness. In a blurr of grace and fierceness, he landed smack on top of Roy Peterson, knocking a mortified Hal to the ground from the powerful blow. Screams filled the night mixed with low guttural growls. My throat ached and strained and I realized the screams were mine. Terrified I watched the heap of fur and man. A whirring sound jolted me to silence. Rapidly it came closer and louder. The Anderson's lights were on now and headlights were approaching. Men in white, holding fiery torches loomed over the cab of a truck. Their heads ringed in halos of light.

"Oh Lord, No!" I cried, and began to bolt. The fire, the torches, "Not them. Not now," I said aloud. A long barrel pointed towards us from the back of the truck. "Jesus!" I closed my eyes. They were close enough I could hear the slide of the barrel. Falling to the ground I wished the black pavement would swallow me up. There came a noise so deafening it caused my ears to ring and Brutus gave out with a yelp. Opening my eyes I could see the lion trying to run, only to slump to the pavement beneath him after a few yards. Roy Peterson lay in a huddled lump, and Hal was standing over his father. The men with the torches had left the pickup and were gathered 'round Roy Peterson and Brutus.

Buddy must be frantic by now. I had to get help. Seeing my opportunity I managed to pick myself up and I lit out for home. I fixed my sights on the porch lights ahead and..."Cally!" a large hand came crashing down on my arm from behind. I tried to scream, but nothing came out.

"Whoa! Cally, where you running off to like a scared rabbit? Hold on there," Jack Jackson's voice said sending a calm over my trembling insides. Turning towards the voice, Jack Jackson's face illuminated in torchlight was a hellava welcome sight. "You're shaking like a leaf Cally," Jack Jackson said pulling my now limp and washed out body close to him. I hung on to him for dear life. Big crocodile tears streamed down my cheeks as relief ran through my body. Sheriff Baines' patrol car drove up, his headlights glaring on the Clyde Beatty Circus logo written across the side of the pickup. Workers in white jackets with the same logo on their backs loaded Brutus into the back of the truck. Jack Jackson just stood there his enormous arms wrapped around me; their velvety hairs softly tickling my face. The Sheriff called on his radio for an ambulance.

"Mr. Jackson," I said looking up and wiping my eyes, "You'd better tell them to send two ambulances. He looked questioningly." I said, "There's been some awful trouble down to the cemetery."

"Who's hurt Cally," he asked anxiously. My words poured out, "Bud's friend Larry is real bad hurt and I think a man by the name of Zeke is dead. He's a friend of Roy Peterson. He's mean, real mean Mr. Jackson. Him and Mr. Peterson was gonna' hang the colored man, Isaac, and probably shoot my brother Bud and his friend Larry. Zeke shot at me and Hal."

"Holy shit!" Jack Jackson said his expression fearful and full of concern, "Sheriff, we got bigger trouble. You better get two ambulances, and don't let Peterson out of your sight. Not that he's going anywhere."

Jack Jackson picked me up and sat me on the truck's tailgate telling me to sit tight. He and the Sheriff talked by the patrol car. Pretty directly, the Sheriff started up his car, lights on and took off toward the cemetery. Another patrol car drove up and one man got out and went over to where Roy Peterson was. Jack Jackson told me to come on and get in the patrol car. I climbed in with Mr. Jackson behind me. He told the driver, "Let's get this young lady home Pete." As Pete turned the car around Jack Jackson ruffled the hair on top of my head. I flinched with pain as he touched my forehead. Pulling my bangs back to have a better look, Jack Jackson gave out with a whistle, "Man alive Cally where in blue blazes did you get that goose-egg?"

"I must've hit the wind shield harder than I thought," I said flinching again as my hand automatically went to the spot.

"What windshield, Cally?" the Deputy asked.

"The one in the Grey Ghost when Hal and I wrecked it," I told him.

Well, right quick, the patrol car came to a screeching stop and I could feel four eyes burning right through me. I thought I best start explaining, so I began my condensed version of the night's events. The two men sat mesmerized as I spoke, and if it hadn't been for the sirens they'd have never noticed the ambulances racing by. All the deputy kept doing was shake his head and repeating every once in a while "Well I'll be damned."

When I'd finished Jack Jackson said, "Come on Pete, let's get her home. She's had one hell of an evening, and it ain't over yet."

The Jackson house was lit up like an old man's birthday cake when we pulled in the drive. The back door opened and all hell broke loose. Everyone was talking at once except for Kate and Lynn, who for once in their lives seemed speechless. We got out of the patrol car and Jack Jackson's voice boomed through the confusion. There came a welcome silence.

"What's going on Jack?" Dad demanded.

"She's all right. Just a little shook up, but you better come with me and Pete here. Bud needs you. He's down at the colored cemetery." Glancing at my mom he said, "He's all right Kathryn, but there's been some trouble and we need to get down there right away. You might want to take Cally in and lie her down. She's got a nasty bump on the head." At that Mom put her arm around my shoulder and walked me into the house with Lynn, Kate and Gloria following. The deputy's car pulled out the drive as we shut the door. As soon as we hit the light of the kitchen the look in Mom's face turned to concern as she brushed my hair back.

"Sit your sister down Kate, I'm calling the Doc," Mom ordered, her voice noticeably shaken.

In the living room Kate looked like she'd bust a gut with curiosity and the wonderful silence was broken.

"What in Sam Hill have you got into now Cally Cummins? What's happened to Buddy? What's he doing down at the cemetery?" Kate went on and on and my head started feeling like it might explode. I grabbed it and moaned and Lynn told Kate to knock it off. Mom came in complete with ice bag in hand making me lie down. Placing the bag gently on my bump she asked me to tell her what happened. As I spoke the four sat gaped mouthed and the only sound other than my voice was a gasp, or a "good Lord" from Kate every once in a while, which was quickly stifled by Mom with one look. Pretty soon someone was on the front porch and the doorbell rang. Lynn ran over and opened it and Doc Winters came in with his crackly worn black leather bag. He sat it on the coffee table, reached in and pulled out a silver flashlight. I blinked as the pin head light flashed across my eyes.

"Look over here Cally," Doc said moving back and forth.

"Acchh!" I groaned as he touched my bump.

"Hurts pretty bad don't it?" he said.

"Well, doggone it, Doc, if you knew that why'd you go poking at it," I told him.

"Cally!" Mom scolded at my brashness.

"It's a nasty bump, probably a slight concussion, so you'll need to keep ice on it Kathryn, and keep her down," he instructed Mom. Looking over his spectacles at me he said, "If it's possible to keep this young lady down that long. I can't give her much right now with that bump, but I can give her a little something to settle her down," he said pulling the biggest darn needle I'd seen since he tried to give me a polio shot a while back. I had run all over his office then and it took him and his nurse to get me out from under the examining table. I couldn't run now which seemed to delight him as he smiled and made me turn over and bare my back side. It was just a little poke and afterwards Mom wrapped me in the daisy afghan Grandma had made. The cushions were soft like clouds of cotton. My body sunk and molded into them as a flow of warmth ran over me. A nice, warm feeling, safe…

CHAPTER EIGHTEEN

The scent of "Lilly of the Valley", fresh and light filled my nostrils waking me. Mom's green eyes met mine and caressed me. Her drawn, worried lines had disappeared. She smiled softly. The bong of the grandfather clock announced it was one o'clock.

"It'll just take a minute Will. I just need to ask her a few questions to finish up my report. It's pretty clear what went on down there but, I have to ask her," a man was saying as he walked across the room.

Sheriff Baines, his Stetson under his arm stood in front of me. I groggily sat up straight and stared at the man. He was a downright handsome man with brown hair and eyes to match. Much younger looking here in the light of the living room.

"Cally, Sheriff Baines needs to ask you a few questions about what happened tonight," Dad said cautiously.

It wasn't a bad dream after all. It was all rushing back in my head. I was almost afraid to ask, "Daddy is Buddy okay?"

"I'm fine Cal." It was Buddy. "I'm right here," he said walking over and giving me a hug. My eyes welled up. I leaned back and took a good look. He was a sight, shirt torn under the sleeve and his coal black hair all tousled over his eyes. I panicked remembering, "Larry? Isaac?" I stammered.

"They'll be alright Cally. An ambulance came and took Larry to the hospital. The driver said it looked like he had some broken ribs but thought he'd be alright." Reading my eyes, he said, "Really Cal, he's okay." Then Buddy sort of laughed, "He told me to tell you he oughta skin you alive for hiding in the ghost the way you did, but he's awful glad you did. Said to tell you if you were about seven years older he'd marry you someday." I could feel my face warming up, probably red as blazes. Buddy winked.

Suddenly I felt the most gosh awful overpowering guilt coming over me. I looked down at the floor saying, "I'm sorry for wrecking up the ghost Buddy, I…"

"Shush, Don't worry none about the old car, you saved our lives. Who cares about the darned old car anyways," he said looking away.

Oh Buddy, I thought. He loved that old car.

Sheriff Baines interrupted my troubled conscience, "Cally, how 'bout those questions now."

Well, I commenced to repeating the story for about the millionth time tonight. I retraced it all, from hiding in the galloping ghost to driving it through the cemetery. He wrote it all down in his notebook especially when I got to the part about Skinny Zeke holding a gun on Larry, Bud and Isaac, and how he turned it on Hal and me. He said he had all he needed to put Roy Peterson under the jail and maybe put a stop to the so-called River Hunt Club, at least for a while anyways.

"Folks around these parts won't be too tolerant of them boys once this story gets out," the Sheriff said.

Voices drifted in off the front porch. Isaac's smoky tones brought a huge smile to my lips. All eyes turned to the doorway. There a weary Isaac stood, his brown face awash with scruffly white stubble. Jack Jackson followed him inside. Isaac caught my gaze and smiled. He walked over and took my hands in his weathered ones.

"God Bless you child," he said. "I knew there was guardian angels, but I'd never seen one 'til tonight. Lord only knows what would've happened to us if you and that young fella' hadn't lit out in that old grey car. When that one fella started waving that rope of his, I thought sure I wasn't long for this world; then land sakes," he turned to my mom and dad, "You shoulda seen it. Your Cally and that young man drove that car across that cemetery like a bat out of hell." Then turning to Buddy he said, "You done taught her right Buddy boy. Whoo Whee! Child, what a sight it was."

Oh man, talk about a guilty conscience I thought, and spoke not looking Isaac square in the eyes, "About your cemetery, with all your kin folk in it and all…Isaac I'm real sorry. I tore it up pretty bad. You don't suppose I made any of them spirits mad do you?"

Isaac grinned that pumpkin grin, "Lawd youngin' the look on those devil's faces when that first tombstone went flying was enough to redeem yourself to the spirits, plus my life being spared…Oh no child. I believe that will be plenty enough to pacify them. Thank you Cally."

"Don't go thanking me, Isaac," I said, not feeling too comfortable taking all the credit. "I believe we're even in the life saving area. It was you stopped Skinny Zeke. Buddy told us what you did. Why Buddy said you moved quicker than a wiry cat with a bunch of dogs after him. He said you didn't miss a beat slammin' clean into that skinny maniac knocking him into the ground. Sorry to say I missed it, but I did hear the shattering blast. It sounded like a cherry bomb going off and…" I looked at Isaac's face and stopped running on so. He didn't look so good and he sank heavily into the ottoman in front of Dad's chair.

"You all right Isaac?" I said touching his shoulder. He didn't speak. He just stared at the brown and gold hook rug on the floor.

"Oh no, Isaac," I said understanding. "Now don't you go feeling poorly about all that gun stuff," I said looking to Buddy for a little help here.

Buddy cleared his throat and said, "It was an accident. He fell on his own gun. It was his own fault Isaac. It could've been us lying there if you hadn't done what you did."

Bud's words didn't seem to help much. Isaac was a good, decent man involved in another man's dying. It would be hard to take even if it was a no good creep like Zeke that got his life snuffed like a candle. Shoot I could hardly believe it. Skinny Zeke was dead. I'd seen it, it was real enough, but he was so full of meanness I didn't figure anybody like that would ever die. But, the man was dead, right down the road. A man I'd heard talk and breathe and now he was dead in the colored cemetery. How he hated them colored people, and now his evil spirit was amongst them. A chill ran down my spine.

Isaac sat staring into his folded hands that hung down between his knees.

"It's alright Mr. Washington," Sheriff Baines said. "Those men can't be causing you or these children anymore trouble. Not anymore." That didn't seem to ease Isaac's pain.

Mom brought Isaac a cup of steaming coffee. He accepted it with a grateful nod. I couldn't help smiling watching the sweet old gentleman huddled over, blowing and sipping his coffee. I recalled two girls scaring one another with stories of a crazy old colored man. A man wielding a six-inch switchblade ready to chop up any little kid crossed his path and use them for bait.

Jack Jackson interrupted my reflecting. "Mr. Washington, I been thinking." Isaac looked up swallowing a cooled gulp. "Will here tells me he's moving the family to the new house in a couple weeks. I've been milling it over in my mind and I think I just might move back into this house. Maybe get the grove producing like it did years back. Maybe even get myself some more hives going. If I do I'm going to need some help. Someone to keep an eye on the workers when I'm gone to my other job." Isaac studied the big man as he continued, "I'd fix up that old garage out back. Thought I could turn it into a little cottage for you if you stay on as my foreman. Of course, you'd have to help do the work, I ain't offering no charity you understand."

Isaac smiled and raised his eyebrows and then he spoke real hesitantly, "I don't know Mr. Jackson. I'm not so sure I want to stay in these parts after all that's happened." He rubbed a hand through salt and pepper hair, "I was thinking maybe I'd go up to Ocala. Maybe look up my nephew that owns a bait shop up on Wildcat Lake. Maybe he'd give me a job."

"You don't have to go deciding right now, but at least let me put you up for a while 'til you think on it," Jack Jackson offered.

Isaac kept studying Jack Jackson. Then after some coaxing from Bud, he gratefully accepted the offer to stay a while 'til he made up his mind what he'd do. With that agreed upon Jack Jackson said he figured it was high time he and Isaac went on home and let us good people get off to bed.

With that Sheriff Baines took his leave too. Dad stopped Isaac on his way out and told him if there was anything he needed not to hesitate asking. "You helped save my kids and for that I'm forever beholding to you Mr. Washington," Dad said a hand on Isaac's shoulder.

"Yes, and I expect you both for dinner next Sunday," Mom told them.

Everyone said their goodnights.

Later as we were all getting settled in our beds, the house grew quiet. Quiet, that is, except for the floorboards creaking in the hallway as Mom and Dad walked by each room saying their goodnights. I closed my eyes and listened to them and savored every sweet goodnight until I heard their door creak shut at the end of the hall. Wrapped securely beneath the covers next to Lynn I opened my eyes and stared through the panes in the window. Starlight filled the darkness like a thousand cat's eyes glowing in the night.

I tried to shake it, but Hal Peterson kept crossing my mind. A little tinge of guilt unnerved me as I lay so safe and warm and loved. I wondered what would become of Hal now that his daddy was a jailbird. Hopefully, Roy Peterson's evil hadn't been too contagious so as not to pass from father to son. Hal had some good in him. I'd seen it tonight. Bits and pieces of a scripture passage started buzzin' in my head. 'An evil man'…What was it? Darn, I could never remember them. Patty probably would know. Lord, she could spout them out for just about any occasion. It could be real aggravating sometimes, especially when it was a guilt concocting one kept me from doing something I wanted to. I wasn't one for quoting or remembering verses too well. What was it?

"An evil man out of the evil"…That was it. "An evil man out of the evil treasure of his heart bringeth forth that which is evil." Gosh, poor Hal. That one doesn't leave much hope for the offspring of such a father like Roy Peterson. Surely Hal could change. He was young. Afterall, circumstances sure had changed me these past few months. So much had changed…It was real scary how one day a body could be carefree and without a worry in the world and then the next day that world could turn completely upside down. Oh sure, maybe a kid might have little worries like if Miss Rowell was feeling particularly ornery one day and went and sprung a pop test on us. Or, maybe a bad day being one where you got stuck having to pick slow as molasses, Melissa Barker on your kickball team. But, never as I live and breathe could I imagine the things us kids had seen and done since we'd moved here in this big white house. I knew I'd never look at things quite the same as I had last summer or the times before. We'd seen a whole different kind of world now. We were just kids, but somehow I didn't feel like it anymore. In time, this fall and this place would be a distant memory to me; not one I'd likely forget, or should, even if I wanted to, but still a memory. It would sort of float hauntingly back, like one of them ghostly spirits in the colored cemetery, haunting and frightening my brother Bud and me. We may never speak of it again, but there it will be just the same. We'd know what the other knew. I felt closer to my brother now more than ever.

I closed my eyes. Skinny Zeke's face, stone cold dead, flashed my mind. My eyes were wide open now. I whispered "Dear Lord, how many more are out there like him?" Lynn mumbled, startling me. I pulled the covers up tight, snuggling closer to my sister. Out the window a big charcoal cloud passed over the stars and from the the tall pine I could hear the spooky old hoot owl. The sandman was working mighty hard dusting my eyelids. They felt heavier and heavier. I'll think on all these things tomorrow. Things always seemed more hopeful in the light of day.

ABOUT THE AUTHOR

Colleen Affeld was born in Pennsylvania, one of five children of the Wharry family. The family moved to Florida when she was four years old. It was there she grew up in the grove dotted landscapes of central Florida near the St. John's river. The area is full of great beauty and southern charm. In an area well known for its tourism with all its glitz and entertainment, just a short drive away is this river country. It remains a hidden gem, the real Florida in all its tropical splendor; gators, tropical birds, and manatee sharing the river's ecosystem. So, it was about this familiar place that the author chose to write this fictional tale of suspense, intrigue and danger. Like the boil bubbling from the sandy bottoms of the many area springs, the area conjures up past images just waiting to be written about. A new author, Ms. Affeld has many more tales to tell about this land of her youth. The author has now made her home in Northwest Indiana with her husband, Keith, and daughter Deanna. She also has a son, Jim and two daughters, Kerri and Wendy, six grandchildren and a seventeen year old cat named Squeakie. She has worked for Dining Services at Valparaiso University for the past twenty years and over the last several years has studied her craft of writing there. Someday in the near future she and her family plan on spending at least part of their time back in the warmth of the Florida sunshine.

I read "The Grey Ghost" with pleasure. I find it a fine offering for young adult fiction with believable characters the reader can identify with. The character of Bud Cummins, big brother of our narrator, nine-year old Cally gives the reader a sense of leadership with his level-headedness. Bud sharpens Cally's character, who brings the adventure to the story. Isaac Washington, the siblings new found older friend is goodness in a world of evil, patience under pressure, the pure milk of human kindness, a gentle and believable figure. This is a genuinely comforting tale, not unlike the books I read (and depended on) as a kid: the Hardy Boy series, the Motor Boy series, etc.

Walter Wangerin, Jr.
American Book Award Winning Author